Georgiana

Sherri Beth Johnson

DEDICATION

To my husband Jared, my beautiful daughter Victoria, and my
miracle man Zane. I dreamt of you since I was a little girl, and I am
so thankful God gave me each of you!
You are my dreams come true!

CONTENTS

Other Books By Sherri Beth Johnson

The Andley Sisters Series, Farmers Daughters

Georgiana, Book One

Valynn, Book Two

Genevieve, Book Three

Augusta, Book Four

The Kenrick Brides Series

Charleigh, Book One

The Royals of Gliston Series

Estelle, Book One

Taisia, Book Two

Anne of Fales, Book Three

Gracelyn, Book Four

Cairistiona, Book Five

Gemma, Book Six

ACKNOWLEDGMENTS

I first want to thank my Heavenly Father and Jesus Christ for gifting me this book series. I want to thank my family for supporting me, for eating cereal and grilled cheese too often, and for ignoring my moods as they changed along with my characters by the minute. I want to thank my friend Keri Lynn for believing in me and encouraging me. I want to thank my editors, Ms. Cora, my sweet friend Ramona, and my dear friend Lora, for all their hard work and support. I want to thank my mother and mother-in-law for being my cheerleaders. For my beautiful daughter Victoria, thank you for being my inspiration. And to my little miracle man Zane, you inspire me to never give up, for it is through your life that I have been forced to dig deeply within myself. And last, but not least, I want to thank my husband Jared for choosing me, for being my forever love story, and for holding my hand on this wild ride we call life. I adore you!

PROLOGUE

I sat on the front pew in the little country church I had
attended my entire childhood. My stomach rolled and sweat
beaded upon my forehead as I nervously watched the couple
standing before Pastor Crawley, pledging their lives to one
another in Holy Matrimony. It was my best friend Eleanor
Bentley and her beau Matthias Stein, just one of the four
couples that would be wed this hot July morning. I swallowed
hard as I attempted to look over my sister Celia's shoulder,
where across the aisle the grooms waited their turns; there he
sat, Keane Kenrick, my intended. As if he could read my mind,
he looked at me, his face unreadable, but I knew he did not
want me for a wife; he loved another. Tears threatened to slip
from my eyes as I quickly began to fan myself, willing some
kind of air to my person, lest I faint. What a mess I found
myself in, and it was all Keane's fault, well, at least most of it
was his fault.

I closed my eyes, praying for God to deliver me from this fate,
and I felt my sister Celia, just two years younger than I, squeeze
my arm tenderly. "Do not worry so, Georgie! It will all work
out," she whispered tenderly. I looked at my younger sister; she
was the sole reason I was sacrificing my life to a loveless
marriage. Her hazel eyes revealed her happiness; her sweet
cherub face glowed with the same bridal bliss that Eleanor's
did. It was a bliss I would never understand, but I would do
anything to make my sister happy. I loved her this much,
enough to marry a man who could not stand the sight of me,
just so she and her beau John Stein could wed, and so I could
obtain my own farm. A future.

I am the oldest of five daughters, born to Alvin and Margaret
Andley, farmers. At twenty years of age, I was nearly a spinster,

2

and my father's beliefs demanded that the oldest daughter wed before the younger ones. But I had received no suitors; no man was interested in me. Once, at sixteen, a young man had seemed to like me, but his family had sold their farm and moved into the city. We had written to one another for several months, and then, his letters had ceased to come. I was heartbroken for a while, but life on the farm kept me busy enough that eventually I had resolved in my heart my lot in life—an unwanted spinster.

As the Pastor announced Matthias and Eleanor man and wife, they took their seats together in the reserved pew behind me as everyone smiled and clapped in congratulatory fashion. I wrung my handkerchief nervously. Would Keane and I be called next? His eyes met mine; his face was pale, and he quickly looked straight ahead as if he was being sentenced to death.

"Would Drew Weston and Millicent Smythe please join me?" Pastor Crawley called. I could not help but let out a loud sigh of relief, causing Celia to blush and give me a most stern look. I did not care. Everyone knew the story around my impending marriage; they all knew it was not a love match but an arranged marriage by Mr. and Mrs. Kenrick, Keane's grandparents. I looked behind me to the side, several rows back where my parents sat smiling with Keane's grandmother, Adeline Kenrick, sitting beside them with a wistful sort of look on her face. Didn't she know she was destroying two lives this day? She caught me watching her and she simply nodded a silent encouraging nod. I gave her a weak smile and turned to watch as Millicent and Drew said their vows. Out of four couples being united this day, mine and Keane's was the only loveless match. I closed my eyes and went back to that day just a week ago, the day that forever changed my life....

Chapter One

I stood outside the large, two story farmhouse, admiring the pink and white peonies lining the front of the large wrap around porch of the Kenrick's home. "If I ever marry, I want a house just as this one," I whispered to myself as I bent down to smell the fragrant blooms.

"Georgie dear, what a pleasant surprise! Come on in out of the heat," Adeline Kenrick called to me from the screen door. I shifted the basket of food I had prepared and smiled as she hugged me in greeting. She welcomed me inside; the scent of cinnamon and apples lingered in the warm air. It was such a lovely home.

"How is Mr. Kenrick doing this morning?" I asked, concerned for our neighbor. His health had been in terrible decline over the last month and the older couple anxiously awaited family to arrive before his passing. His death seemingly loomed about in this beloved home.

Adeline's blue eyes filled with tears as she shook her head negatively. "I pray our grandson arrives today; I feel Jorik is only waiting for him," she said softly.

"My family and I have been praying for his speedy arrival as well," I assured her. My father had led us in bedtime prayers every night for the last month for Jorik Kenrick's family to arrive in time.

"I know you have. You and your family have been true friends and a Godsend. Especially you, Georgie. I look forward to your visits; your lovely smile encourages Jorik and me. You are such

4

a help in the kitchen and on the farm. I can hardly believe a young man has not caught your hand in marriage yet," the older woman said, pouring tea as I set the basket down on the counter in the lovely red and white kitchen I had come to adore.

I blushed and scoffed. "Not for me, not plain old Georgiana Andley. But Celia and Valynn seem to have plenty of offers," I said, feeling my ripe old age of twenty.

Adeline looked shocked. "You are not plain, Georgie, not in the least. Maybe just a bit shyer than your sisters, but your heart is twice the size of theirs put together, and that is where the true beauty lies," Adeline encouraged.

I thanked her softly and sipped my tea. "What can I help you with this morning, Mrs. Kenrick?" I asked. Half an hour later I stood over the boiling cauldron stirring the laundry and feeling like I myself was boiling in the hot July sun. I heard a commotion coming from the front of the house but continued on with my task, figuring that more visitors had come to call on the older couple. Within minutes Adeline came rushing out of the house and called frantically for me to come inside. I quickly left my laundry, rushed inside and followed her to the large bedroom downstairs where Mr. Kenrick lay. My footsteps slowed as I realized he must have passed. But upon entering the room, I saw a handsome young man sitting on the side of the bed, holding the older man's hand in his and weeping. My heart ached at the sight, but as I heard Mr. Kenrick speak in a soft and fading voice, I realized his time had not yet come.

"This is Keane, our grandson," Adeline whispered to me. Jorik motioned for Adeline to come to him; she leaned over the bed to be able to hear her husband's request.

She turned to me and spoke. "Georgie, run home quickly and bring your father. Take one of our horses, but go quickly and return," she pleaded.

I nodded and fled the room, wondering why Mr. Kenrick would need my father; he was simply a farmer, not a doctor or Pastor. I wasn't the best rider and horses made me a little nervous, but I found Henry, the hired hand, out in the barn and he quickly helped me onto what he promised was his tamest horse. I rode home praying all the way for God's protection.

I found my father behind our house sharpening the tools for the upcoming harvest. After quickly relaying Mr. Kenrick's request, my father saddled our own mare and followed me back to the Kenrick's farm. Father was a quiet and reserved man. He and Mr. Kenrick had been neighbors for fifteen years and had helped one another with spring plantings and the harvest each year. I watched my father's concerned face as he gently removed his hat and greeted Mrs. Kenrick. I knew that this older man's passing would deeply affect my father; they were good friends despite their age difference.

"Alvin, Jorik and I need to speak with you, Georgiana, and Keane. We have been waiting anxiously for Keane's arrival, and now that he has finally arrived, we have no time to waste," she said, twisting her apron in her hands. Jorik Kenrick nodded for his wife to go ahead and speak as he took her hand in his, willing her the last of his strength.

"In all the years we have been neighbors, Alvin, your family has been our family. You have helped us every planting, every harvest, and any time in between that we needed you. Your wife and Georgiana have cooked for us so many times, have cleaned our home and visited with us. Our own children are spread across this continent. Our oldest son Jaffett, Keane's father, has a much larger and much more prosperous farm than we. He has no interest in our small place. We have asked Keane to come for over a year now, and finally he has arrived. Jorik and I have prayed for a year now, and we feel this is the best way and God's will. Keane, you are our grandson and rightful heir to Kenrick Farms, but it is only by marrying Georgiana that you will inherit it. You might be our blood heir, but this young woman and her father's blood, sweat, and tears are in this land and house. They have taken care of us when none of our family dared come help us. You two will marry and both own equal parts of the land and house," Ms. Adeline said firmly.

I gasped in utter shock. My knees nearly gave out beneath me as Father clasped my hand in his to keep me from speaking just yet. I looked over to see Keane's face red in anger. This must be a devastating blow to him, I thought silently. My father looked down at me with a thoughtful look, but I shook my head no, I didn't want to marry this man.

"Jorik and Adeline, this is a very thoughtful gift. I assure you we have done these tasks with only love in our hearts, never expecting anything in return. Georgiana has a big heart and has come to love you both like the grandparents she never had. Perhaps we should discuss this in the hallway and let you speak with your grandson alone," my father said as he gently pushed me into the carpeted hallway, shutting the door behind him. My heart raced so fast I sank down in a chair outside the door. Had I not just wished out loud that I would have a house such as this one day?

"Georgie, I think you must accept Jorik and Adeline's offer. You are twenty years old and have no other prospects. It is as if God himself designed this. You will own land, your farm will adjoin ours, and you will be close enough to visit your mother and sisters. And when your own children come along, your mother will be close enough to help. This is a grand farm,

Georgie; you will have this beautiful house," he whispered excitedly.

I swallowed hard and nodded. I loved this farm, just as I loved Jorik and Adeline. I had helped out around their place so much it felt like a second home to me. But from the look of their grandson's face, he was not happy to share his inheritance with me. "But I do not know him," I whispered nervously. A raised voice could faintly be heard through the solid wood door, and I heard Keane speaking to his grandparents.

"But I cannot marry her, Mormor! I love another; her name is Melody and she lives in my hometown. We plan to wed this fall!" he insisted angrily. My father's blue eyes met my own and I cringed knowing that my fate lay in the hands of this angry man just inside the door.

"I am sorry, Keane, but this is our demand. If you wish to inherit this farm as your own, you will marry Georgiana. She is a dear sweet girl. She is a wonderful Christian and cooks better than I. She has the biggest heart and knows a lot about farming. She will be a great asset to you. She has worked this place for years and deserves this farm more than you," Adeline insisted.

"And what about love, Mormor? Would you have me deny my heart and live with a woman I do not love for the rest of my life?" he asked again, raising his voice.

I raised my chin higher and Father patted my cheek tenderly. "What are your feelings, daughter?" Father asked me softly.

I shrugged. It was too much to take in. "I suppose if I marry, then Celia and John will no longer have to wait on me. And I do love this farm," I whispered nervously.

Father smiled and nodded. "Celia and John would be very thankful," he whispered, knowing his next to oldest daughter had pleaded for six months to marry her beau John Stein, but Alvin firmly believed Georgie must marry first, being the oldest and approaching the age where no one would want her.

"But did you see her?" I heard Keane hiss. "She is plain and backward. If you only met Melody you would love her just as much as this girl. Will you not give me time to bring her here?" he begged.

Tears formed in my eyes and my father kissed my cheek. "He is hurt and angry, Georgie; he will not allow himself to see how lovely you are," Father tried to assure me, but I knew Keane spoke the truth. I was plain with dark blonde hair and blue eyes, with a smidge of freckles across my nose. There was nothing lovely about me. I was thin and petite, and next to Celia's curvy figure and auburn hair and Valynn's pale blonde hair and large blue eyes, I was quite plain and quiet.

"Please, can we just go home?" I asked, not able to hold back my tears now.

"No, I want this farm for you, Georgie; we will stay and fight for it," Father said firmly.

I sat defeated, feeling quite ugly and smelly from the hot July sun and from laboring over the laundry. "Oh the laundry!" I said, standing and rushing away before Father could catch me. Outside I stirred the pot, thankful for the steam to hide my tears. Keane Kenrick was a very rude man.

Nearly an hour later Father found me outside, hanging the wash on the clothes line. By now the sun was starting to set, and I knew we would need to return home to do the milking and chores I helped with each day.

"Keane has agreed to wed. I am heading home to do the choring, but in the morning I will send Pastor Crawley out to speak with Jorik and Adeline. They want the wedding to take place within a week's time. I think Jorik is hanging on until he knows it is settled. But rest assured, Georgie, half this farm will be yours, daughter, and I am so proud of you. You, out of all my girls, have won Jorik's and Adeline's love and trust. And now I am relieved to see you have a future," Father said smiling.

I could only nod, because a lump the size of a melon felt lodged in my throat. "I will help Adeline lay out supper, and then I will come home to help," I said softly.

Father nodded as he looked at the sun's low position. "Have that future husband of yours drive you home; you need not be walking in the dark," he said concerned. I nodded but knew I would never ask such a thing from a man that called me plain and backwards and who loved another. I kissed Father's cheek goodbye and quickly finished hanging the laundry. I had just lifted the heavy basket to return to the house when I saw *him* standing before me. A scowl marred his handsome face and tension electrified off his being. I raised my chin high. I might be plain, but I was a lady, not a servant, or an imbecile.

As I went to walk around him, he called to me, "Stop! I am sorry. What was your name?" Keane asked.

My face burned crimson. His Mormor, as he called her, had said my name at least four to five times in their conversations and he could not remember my name? My chin lifted higher. "Georgiana Andley," I said softly.

He looked at his feet and kicked a tuff of grass. "Well, Georgiana Andley, how much money will it take to buy you out?" he asked in his cocky attitude.

I gasped. "Whatever do you mean?" I asked, knowing what he meant, but not believing he would even ask it.

"Your share of the farm, how much will it take for you to walk away?" he asked bluntly.

I could feel my cheeks burning red now as I shifted the basket onto my hip. Watching the movement, he frowned, and then yanked the basket from me. I suppose trying his best to be a gentleman, but he wasn't fooling me. "What would I do with money?" I asked.

He laughed bitterly. "Surely you're not as daft as that? Surely you know that kind of money can buy you many things in life. Maybe a few new dresses wouldn't hurt," he said, eyeing my faded blue calico.

I gasped again at his rudeness. "I do not need a few more dresses; I need a home, a husband and security," I said, hating the fact and marching away from him.

But the devil caught up to me with the basket on his shoulder as if it weighed nothing. "I do not want to be that husband," he stated firmly.

I whirled around to him. "I wouldn't want you for my husband if you were the last man on earth! But I do want this farm! I love this place and I love your grandparents. I have become very attached to them over the last fifteen years," I said with tears in my eyes and emotion annoyingly cracking in my voice.

"I, too, love this place! It is my inheritance! I am the second son; my older brother inherits my family farm. Without this farm I have nothing!" he exclaimed. I simply shrugged and kept walking toward the back door praying Mrs. Kenrick would come to my rescue.

"Mormor said you have a big heart, but I can't see it! If you did, you would allow me to buy you out. I could marry my girl back home and have this farm, keep it in my family," he said angrily.

"I do have a big heart! It is big enough that I wish to please your mormor and marry an arrogant idiot just to make her happy. My heart is also big enough to want to marry so my younger sister and her beau can wed. Just because I have no heart for you, doesn't mean I have no heart!" I yelled back.

He growled behind me in frustration as I made it to the back steps. "You could travel anywhere you wanted with the kind of money I would give you," he said desperately.

I frowned. "How could you come up with that kind of money? Is your intended wealthy? Does she too wish to buy this farm?" I asked, not truly caring, and my mind rushing ahead of me. Would Father prefer the money to my marriage? Would the money help him and Mother? Of course it would, but that would leave me a spinster, and this idiot before me my neighbor. I looked around the farm as the sun set. It was the most beautiful sight in the world. My heart ached with wanting for this place.

As I looked at Keane, his head was bowed. "I do not exactly have the money. I would need to see about getting a loan for your half. Melody, well she is a city girl, but she can learn to be a farmer's wife," he insisted.

I realized I had begun to smirk. I quickly frowned. But inside I laughed, wishing I could see him turn his city girl into a farmer's wife, to see her in her silks milking old Gertie the cow, mucking out the horse barn. "Well, I must insist you ask her about the investment; if she is even willing to buy me out," I said, turning to go inside. I was relieved he did not follow me and quickly began to warm supper up on the cook stove. I brought in a load of wood and sat it on the back porch for Adeline, just as she found me.

"I have dinner warmed for you all, but it is getting late and I must head home before dark," I said, hugging this dear woman.

She smiled back and sighed. "Now, if Jorik can hold on a week, you and Keane will make us the happiest grandparents alive," she said wistfully. I gave her a weak smile. Poor Adeline. If Melody agreed to the loan and Keane could obtain it, I would not be her new granddaughter; I would not be living in this lovely farmhouse. Tears filled my eyes as I wished her goodnight. I took up my basket and headed home through the back fields. I had waited too late to leave, as I could barely make out my feet in front of me. I sped up, praying that soon I could see the lights of home to guide me.

"Hey, Georgiana!" I heard and turned around. Keane was saddled on a horse and held a lantern. "What are you doing walking in the dark?" he asked, as if it annoyed him.

"I am going home," I said, turning back and walking once more.

"It is too dangerous out this late by yourself; you'll get lost in these wheat fields," he warned.

I shrugged. "What would you care, Mr. Kenrick?" I asked as I hurried along.

He sighed and stopped his horse. "I am not an ogre, Miss Andley. I am sorry I have been so hard on you. But I had this all planned out in my head, and it isn't working to my plans, no offense to you personally," he said in a most calm voice. I turned and frowned at him, then continued on my path.

13

"You are a stubborn young woman!" he called, urging his mount on behind me.

"Please go away," I begged, turning back to him. My heart ached and my head hurt from holding back my tears and arguing.

"I am sorry, Georgiana, but if you do not get on this horse, I am afraid I must follow you home, one step at a time. And I pray we do not come across any snakes out here in the fields," he said with a grin. It was the first time I had seen him anything but angry, and his handsomeness made my breath catch in my chest. I looked at my feet. He was right; it was silly of me to walk because with the hot sun gone, the serpents would indeed be making their way through these fields, but I loathed the thought of riding with such an arrogant man. I sighed and walked over to him as he slid off the horse and helped me mount. To my surprise, he put me holding the lantern in front of him, not behind him.

As if he knew my thoughts, he softly commented. "If the horse gets spooked, I do not want you on its tail end. I can hold you better up here," he said. I softly thanked him and held my breath lest I lean back against him. He chuckled as if he knew what I was doing but said nothing else until we reached my home. He slid off the horse and took the lantern from me, carefully sitting it on the ground and then lifting his hands to my waist and lifting me off the horse. Because I had sat side saddle for too long, with little to eat all afternoon, my legs buckled underneath me. His strong arms caught me as we came face to face. I was mortified. I must look even worse than before after struggling in the hot sun all afternoon over laundry.

"I will telegraph Melody and my father tomorrow morning. I will also ask the local bank what your part of the place is worth. I have a little money saved, but I know it is not enough. Can I call on you tomorrow evening to let you know what I find out?" he asked, his blue eyes searching mine.

I merely nodded. He mounted his horse and I could not help but ask. "It is a small farm; your grandfather has been unable to plant on the majority of the land for years now. This harvest will be small; can you make the payments on the place if you take out a loan?" I asked. I shouldn't care if he got into debt and lost the place, but somehow I had asked before thinking.

"I will make certain before I do anything," he assured me. I nodded and wished him a goodnight. He waited until I was in the front door before he left.

Once inside, I heard giggling and found all four of my sisters peeking out the windows, trying to get a glimpse of the man they all by now thought I was to marry. But the only problem was I wasn't so certain he would marry me.

CHAPTER TWO

As I quickly ate a bite to eat, I explained Keane's plan to my mother and father. Mother started crying and Father shook his head angrily. "I thought you might be pleased; the money could help open up new fields to plant or secure our future," I said softly.

Father shook his head. "We do well, Georgie. Our farm is paid for, and we have money in the bank. We are not wealthy, but we want for nothing. You need this, daughter. What good is the money for your sake? To know you have a husband to care for you, provide for you, give you children is what we want for you," he said sighing.

Tears filled my eyes. "And that I will never have. No one wants me. Not even for a farm free of mortgage. You heard Keane yourself, Father; he is engaged to another. He finds me plain and backward. At least take the money to help buffer the burden I will be for you in my spinster years," I said, rushing away to the room I shared with Celia.

"Georgie, whatever is wrong?" she asked, rising from her bed where she sat sewing. I could not tell her. I could not break her heart, not yet, not just mere hours after she learned she was now free to wed. I shook my head and climbed into bed, not bothering to bathe or undress; I was weary and mentally exhausted. I found I didn't even have the strength to pray.

The next day I did my chores quickly. Mother went to check on the Kenrick's in my place, understanding the less I saw Keane, the better. Father had gone into town and I heated water on the stove for a bath. After a good long soak and a few tears, I dressed in one of my church dresses, a summery lilac dress with white lace underlay. If Keane came to give me news, at least he would see me clean and dressed nicely. Celia sat curling my long dark blonde hair and listened to my retelling of the day before. Tears streamed down her face as I assured her once I had the money, I would insist on Father letting her and John marry. It wasn't fair to my four sisters if I could not obtain a suitor. I moved to the parlor and worked on the mending while I nervously watched the clock on the mantle, wondering just what my future held. My younger sisters, Genevieve and Augusta, joined me with their embroidery as Valynn and Celia worked quietly in the kitchen on Celia's new dress.

It seemed like hours later when I heard the wheels of a buggy pulling up in front of the house as my sisters nervously gathered in the parlor around me. "If he says one thing about you looking plain in that dress, he will deal with all of us," Celia said, stomping her tiny foot upon the carpet and making me smile. I patted her hand and asked that they leave me alone. I didn't want my dear sisters to hear the harshness of Keane's words. It was enough that his words had hurt me the day before; I didn't need witnesses for my heartache and humiliation.

But the person on the other side of the door was not Keane, nor my father, but Pastor Crawley and his wife Miriam. "Good, Georgiana! You need to come with me at once to the Kenrick's farm; your mother and father are both there. Bring your sisters if you like, but we must hurry," he urged. My sisters quickly hurried out the door with me, and I let eleven year old Augusta sit with the Pastor and Miriam while the rest of us crowded the back seat of the buggy.

I had no idea what had happened, but Celia looked hopeful. "I prayed all would turn out all right, Georgie, and I know God heard me," she whispered tenderly.

"And I prayed that city girl would break off their engagement and he would marry you," Valynn whispered mischievously. Celia and I both gasped at our bold sister, but Valynn merely smiled, a very mature sixteen year old. And she felt no guilt, I was certain. I closed my eyes as I remembered the gentler side of Keane on the ride home just the night before. What if he agreed to marry me? Could he be kind? Could we find some kind of mutual companionship? At that moment I doubted it very much.

Once we arrived at the Kenrick's, we were met in the parlor by Father, Mother, and Keane. Pastor Crawley and his wife took their seats on the sofa, as did my sisters in various chairs about the room. "Father, what has happened?" I asked softly, afraid Jorik had passed on. I looked over to find Keane looking me up and down, and I felt a hot blush on my cheeks and ignored him. Was he judging me? Comparing me to his precious Melody? I found myself jealous, and I hated it. What was it about this man that made me so angry and evil?

Father looked to Keane. Keane nervously cleared his throat. "My grandfather has taken a turn for the worse; he could pass on any minute now. He has begged me to marry now, this moment, so he can witness before his death," he said emotionally.

I simply stared at him, my heart frozen in fear, wondering what he intended to do. "What about Melody and the loan?" I asked softly. I heard my mother suck in her breath and prayed she would not go into hysterics.

Keane's blue eyes found mine and he shook his head no. "Even if she would agree to come, the demand is that you share this farm with me, Georgiana. It can never be mine if I marry another," he said just above a whisper.

I nodded in understanding, but several seconds of awkward silence followed.

"Will you consider marrying me, Georgiana Andley, and sharing this farm with me?" he asked nervously.

I looked to my father, and he gave me a weak smile and nodded. "Could I speak with Keane alone in the kitchen?" I asked with tears filling my eyes.

"We must hurry," Keane argued, but instead I grabbed his hand and pulled him into the kitchen, shutting the door behind us. "I am sorry for the way I treated you yesterday. You have no idea how badly I feel," he stammered.

I nodded though I doubted his sincerity. "Good, because I will never in my life be spoken to like that again, Keane Kenrick. Do you understand me?" I asked furious, and so afraid I thought I might lose my lunch all over him.

"If you will marry me, I promise, no matter how much you aggravate me, to respect you. I am not a mean person," he vowed.

My eyes met his and somehow I could see he was sincere. I breathed in deeply. Perhaps Father had been right; perhaps Keane had been acting out of fear and desperation yesterday. "I have a condition to this marriage should I agree," I said, turning my back to him.

"What is your condition?" he asked softly.

"That you will be faithful to me for all time; that you will break your engagement, and never write to Melody again, or speak her name in my presence. I will not be made a fool of, Keane," I said firmly.

The room was too quiet. Perhaps I had asked too much of him? Warm hands were suddenly on my shoulders, gently turning me around to face him. "When I say vows before God, and my grandparents, I promise you to always keep them. I will never dishonor you with another and I will take care of you," he said tenderly, his sacrifice so clearly displayed in his eyes. He would do the honorable thing though his heart was not in it. I almost felt bad for him but nodded in agreement. "I must confess, Georgiana, I am still in love with Melody; it will take time for me to forget her and the life we planned. I ask for patience," he said, looking away from me.

I nodded once again. "I can be patient," I vowed.

He gently took my hand. "So are you agreeing to be my wife?" he asked in a whisper.

I nodded, thankful for my long skirts that hid my trembling knees, unused to having a man hold my hand. "I am," I whispered in return.

There were legal documents that both Keane and I had to sign before we wed. Pastor Crawley stood witness to them, signing below our names. We stood beside the bed hand in hand as Pastor Crawley performed the marriage ceremony for the sake of Mr. Kenrick, who I wasn't certain knew that we were even there. Pastor Crawley insisted we would still need to be wed in the church, but for Jorik's sake, we would marry now so he could pass on in peace. The thought of losing Jorik Kenrick brought me to tears, and I prayed he felt peace as he left this world. He was a dear man to me. Keane's warm hand gently squeezed mine, and I looked up surprised as he nodded to the smile on his grandfather's face. I smiled and thought of the mess I found myself in at that moment; at least I was making someone happy. I could not hold back my tears but let them freely flow down my cheeks, not caring what Keane thought. The rings had not yet been bought, but Adeline quickly handed us hers and Jorik's wedding rings to use until Keane could purchase new ones. I swallowed hard as I felt him slide the cool gold metal over my finger and in a warm voice he pledged to me his vow. When I went to speak, I found I hardly could for my tears, but my mother nodded me on, wiping tears of her own.

"With the power vested in me, I pronounce you husband and wife; you may now kiss your bride," Pastor Crawley said with a tender smile. I froze. Surely Keane would not kiss me, not when he loved another. My father looked at him sternly and suddenly warm lips pressed quickly to mine. He pulled away and our eyes met as I blushed and looked away, terrified I might see revulsion in his eyes, for surely he compared my inexperienced kiss to Melody's. If he hadn't been so mean and arrogant to me, I might have even liked his kiss, which was my very first. I was terrified that his mean and insensitive side would again show once Jorik passed on.

My mother and father kissed me goodnight and Keane assured them he would drive me home. I had not packed my things and was not ready to move into this house. Although our marriage was legal, Pastor Crawley suggested we wait to live with one another until after the church ceremony planned for a week away; however, our wedding certificate was signed and our true wedding date recorded.

We sat around Jorik's bed as Adeline relived hers and Jorik's wedding day nearly fifty years ago in Sweden. I could not help but cry and noticed Keane wiping away a tear himself. It was as if we all sat, reliving the memories, hoping that somehow they might revive Jorik. The hour was getting late, and I went down to the kitchen and prepared a light supper for everyone. We ate in the dining room as Pastor Crawley and Keane talked of crops and the upcoming harvest.

"Three more couples have come to me wanting to marry before harvest. I have set up this Sunday, the twenty-eighth, for the ceremony. We will then share a fellowship banquet afterwards instead of individual receptions. Eleanor and Millicent, as well as your sister, will be joining you as brides, Georgie," Pastor Crawley said. I was happy to hear that Celia would be wed within a week's time.

Suddenly Keane smirked and choked back a laugh. I raised an eyebrow in question. "What did you call my wife?" Keane asked amused, as chill bumps covered my arms at being called his wife.

Pastor Crawley looked to me bewildered. "Georgie?" he said carefully. Keane nodded as he fought back laughter but said nothing more.

I quickly cleared the dishes as Miriam and Pastor Crawley came and hugged me goodnight. "Thank you for dinner, Georgie, it was wonderful as always. I have always said whoever is lucky enough to take you to wife would get the best cook in Lowe County," Pastor Crawley said, making me blush. I thanked them both and saw them to the door.

Ms. Adeline came in from checking on Jorik and kissed my cheek. "Now just because Pastor Crawley thinks you need to wait until Sunday to move in here, you know you're welcome anytime. I love our visits and miss your smile when you are away," she said with tears in her eyes. I nodded and hugged her tightly, feeling her loss even though it had yet to happen.

"I will drive Georgiana home, Mormor, and hurry back," Keane said tenderly.

"Wait! Could I say goodnight to Mr. Kenrick?" I asked, suddenly feeling it was very important to do so.

"I will take her in," Keane said as Mormor nodded with a smile.

I entered the room that felt as if death were already present. I leaned down and whispered, "Goodnight, Mr. Kenrick. Thank you for gifting me your farm. I promise to always love it and take care of it, and I will take care of Ms. Adeline as well. I love you," I said, kissing his forehead as my tears hit his cheek. I gently wiped them away, and he smiled and nodded. As Keane walked me out to his horse, he softly thanked me.

"For what?" I asked.

He had tears in his eyes when he spoke. "For loving them so much."

I had to look away, but nodded. "They are so easy to love," I said emotionally, as he lifted me onto the front of his horse once again. I held the lantern for him as he climbed up behind me. One arm settled around my waist as we headed through the night toward my home. It was bittersweet as I saw the lights of the farmhouse glowing in the distance. In one week this would no longer be where I lay my head, where I sought my comfort and solace.

As Keane lifted me from the horse, he smiled. "Sleep well, Mrs. Kenrick," he whispered. "Or should I call you Georgie?" he asked with a mischievous chuckle.

My face went crimson as I struggled to calm myself down; it was clear he was making fun of my childhood nickname which had always been endearing to me. "It is Georgiana to you. Only those who love me can call me Georgie!" And with that I left him standing in my yard alone in the moonlight.

I struggled to wake as someone gently shook me, whispering my name. My eyes tried to focus, and I found my mother leaning over me. "What is it?" I asked, noticing the room still dark from the night.

"Keane is downstairs waiting. Jorik passed on soon after midnight. Will you go with him?" she asked softly. I nodded and swung my legs over the bed. Celia jumped from her bed and helped me dress by candlelight and I quietly rushed downstairs to find Keane sitting with my father in the kitchen.

If I hadn't known how much he despised me, I would have thought he looked relieved to see me. "Thank you for coming so early. I fear Mormor needs you," he said softly. My mother assured me she and the girls would bring food later in the afternoon and Father would ride into town to see the undertaker as soon as it was daylight. I nodded my head, still foggy with sleep.

Keane led the way to his horse and helped me mount and then swung up behind me. Why he didn't bring the buggy was beyond me, but I sat wishing he had, not wishing to be any closer to him than necessary. We rode slowly, and I felt his arm tighten around my stomach. My face turned bright red as I realized I had leaned back against him and had dozed off.

"Whoa, you nearly tumbled off there. I am sorry to have pulled you from bed so early," he said gently.

"I am fine," I squeaked out and sat up stiffly, causing him to chuckle. I was mortified.

Once in the house, I set about making coffee, hot tea, and breakfast. I did not know how many people would be coming in or out that morning so I thought it best to make several batches of cinnamon rolls. After insisting that Adeline drink a cup of hot tea, I tucked her into the guest bedroom off the parlor and pleaded with her to rest for a few hours.

Alone in the kitchen, I went about my baking. Behind me the door opened and Keane came out of his grandparents' bedroom, his arms full of sheets and quilts, tears in his eyes. I rushed to him. "Let me help you with these," I said softly.

He shook his head no. "You are busy baking, and I need to be out of the house for a bit," he said numbly.

"Shall I help you get the cauldron ready?" I asked searching his face. He shook his head no and left me. Even as I worked in the cheery red and white kitchen, I felt conscious of the dead body on the other side of the door. Sweet Jorik's body, but I knew his spirit was in Heaven although I was still a little afraid. I had never been near a dead body before. Suddenly the uncertainty of what was expected of me this day was overwhelming. I had never handled a funeral; I had no idea what to do.

So I threw myself into baking, frying ham and eggs, and was thankful when Henry and Keane joined me in the kitchen for their breakfast. Henry was taking Jorik's death hard, as he had been their hired hand for twenty years. "After we eat, Henry and I will make the casket. You will come for me if you need me, yes?" Keane asked tenderly.

I nodded. He went to stand and I caught his arm. "I am uncertain what to do," I confided in him nervously.

He surprised me with a gentle smile and patted my hand on his arm. "I am as well, but you are already wise in preparing a large amount of food. We will be overrun with visitors I fear," he said sighing. "Just watch after Mormor, I worry for her." I nodded my head.

After washing the dishes, I went to check on Ms. Adeline. I thought she might be asleep, but I found her looking out the window towards the fields. "Are you hungry, Ms. Adeline?" I asked, hugging her shoulders.

She smiled and shook her head. "I will take another cup of tea though, dear. And please call me grandmother or Mormor as Keane does. You are my granddaughter now," she said with tears in her eyes. I thanked her and rushed to get her tea. I slipped a cinnamon roll onto a plate to try and tempt her to eat something. Then after leaving her, I rushed back into the kitchen to continue my baking, though I jumped at every little noise I heard. I shook my head and chuckled nervously. It isn't as if Jorik would haunt me. I did not believe in ghosts and even if I did, he was too sweet a man to scare me so.

The undertaker arrived with my father shortly after daylight. I was thankful they took the body although it would be returned the next day for burial. I set about scrubbing the bedroom from top to bottom, stopping only to receive the guests that began to arrive to pay their respects to Ms. Adeline and Keane. Pastor Crawley and his wife stayed to help receive the people with Ms. Adeline. I was thankful as I kept busy with the cleaning of the room and keeping the coffee and tea made.

I was hanging the washed linens Keane had started when my mother and sisters arrived. My mother hugged me closely and then frowned. "You look exhausted, Georgie. Valynn has a small bag of clothes for you. Go inside and freshen up. We will set out the food," she said, hugging me tighter. I could not help but cry in her arms; I was overwhelmed and didn't know if I was doing all that needed to be done.

"Georgiana, are you all right?" I heard Keane ask. As Mother released me, I turned my face away; I dried my tears and nodded. My mother quickly ushered the girls into the house with the food. "Are you certain?" he asked softly. I nodded once again. "Come inside and sit down. You have to be exhausted by now," he said, taking my arm and leading me tenderly to the house.

The kitchen was full. My sisters were busily readying the food as Keane pulled out a chair for me and urged me to sit. Mother had a cup of tea and a cinnamon roll for me. "You have already done so much baking, and knowing you as I do, I doubt you ate any of it. No wonder you are worn to a frazzle. But I am proud of you, daughter; you were wise in your decision to bake ahead. I had come to clean the room, but Celia said it had been done and sparkled from top to bottom," she said with worry on her face.

"I wanted it done as soon as possible in case Ms. Adeline wanted to rest in her own room," I said. Keane just sat and stared at me. I realized I was famished and quickly finished my roll and then excused myself to clean up.

Keane led me upstairs to a room that would be mine once I moved in; it sat directly across the hall from the room he had taken. I blushed and thanked him. "No, it is I who need to thank you. I had no idea it took so much work to ready for a funeral. I am done with the casket and will clean up and join you downstairs. I won't leave you until the evening milking," he said as he left me alone. Somehow it made me feel better to know he would be next to me the rest of the day.

By evening the kitchen was full of food; I was thankful for our small community and how they joined together to help. John and Matthias Stein, two of the grooms that would marry the same day as Keane and I, came by. I smiled from a distance as I saw them talking with Keane and trying to befriend him. He was new in town and knew no one except for me and my family.

My mother continued to watch me with concern until they left before the evening milking. "Why don't you come home with us, Georgie? You need to rest," she urged me.

But with one look at Ms. Adeline, I knew I could not leave yet. "Perhaps in a few hours, surely there will not be many more guests to come," I said sighing. Mother hugged me goodbye and I kissed each of my sisters, thanking them for their help. To my surprise, Keane met my family at the back porch and thanked each of them warmly as he helped carry the empty dishes to the carriage. Perhaps he had some manners after all, I thought silently, as I found Ms. Adeline in the parlor.

Pastor Crawley and his wife stood to go, but I quickly urged them to eat supper with us before they left. "You have been here since early morning, please eat before you leave," Ms. Adeline pleaded. Soon they were seated, and I served them just as Keane and Henry came in. Keane immediately set to helping me by serving coffee and tea, and then he firmly ordered me to sit and eat with the others.

"You are lucky to have Georgiana to help you," Miriam Crawley said sweetly as Keane took a seat down the table from me.

He nodded, and without making eye contact with me, he spoke. "I am indeed. I could not have done all of this without her," he said, catching me off guard as my fork fell onto my plate. Blushing, I apologized in time to see him scowl and blush himself. I must have made it obvious that his praise had shocked me and humiliated him in the process. "Forgive him," I told my heart. I could not keep holding this grudge against his earlier actions toward me. He was my husband. I had to forgive him, and I had promised him to have patience.

After the dishes were washed and put away, Pastor Crawley offered to give me a ride home. I looked over to Ms. Adeline. She looked lost and forlorn, but she nodded her approval. "Yes, thank you. I just need to gather my things," I said, rushing towards the stairs.

"No, it is all right, I will see her home," Keane said, surprising me and Ms. Adeline. I stood there; my mouth dropped open wondering why on earth he would offer to drive me when a perfectly good offer of a ride stood in the parlor.

"All right, just do not keep her out late, she looks fatigued," Pastor Crawley said with a wink.

I could feel my cheeks burning as I climbed the stairs to gather my things. When I returned to the parlor, I hugged Ms. Adeline goodnight and asked if she needed anything more. She shook her head no. "I have your room clean and fresh bedding on the bed," I said softly.

Tears filled her eyes. "You are so good to me, my lovely granddaughter. Thank you so much. Will you come back tomorrow?" she asked hopefully.

I nodded. "Of course," I assured her. Keane took my bag and led me out to the stable where Henry readied a horse. I still wondered why he didn't just use the buggy, but allowed him to assist me up in front of him. I held my bag and lantern until he mounted behind me. He wrapped an arm around my waist and slowly walked the horse towards my home.

"I want you to sleep in later in the morning. You have worked hard and need to rest. There is enough food already prepared for Henry and me," Keane said softly. I thanked him and nodded, a new and strange tingling evolved in my stomach at his kindness. I was indeed exhausted and longed to be home, surrounded by my family where I could truly rest. As he took my bag and helped me from his horse, he gently hugged me to him for a brief second and once again thanked me for my help. I bid him a goodnight and went upstairs to my room and sank wearily into bed.

Celia and I arrived at the Kenrick Farm just after breakfast the next morning. I had tried to sleep in, but I was too used to rising with the sun. Dressed in mourning clothes that were stifling in the already warm day, we sat about straightening the kitchen and readying the parlor for the viewing.

I helped Ms. Adeline with her hair; she insisted Keane and I stay with her as the undertaker set up the body in the parlor for the viewing. I had never witnessed such bravery as I did that day from Ms. Adeline.

She kissed her husband's cheek and smiled. "He is no longer suffering; he is completely whole in Heaven with Jesus," she said tenderly. As a sob escaped my throat, I began to fan myself to keep from breaking down at such a sweet sentiment. Keane's arm came around my waist and for some strange reason it comforted me, and I allowed him to keep it there until Celia called for me in the kitchen.

It was another long day of receiving guests who came to pay their respects. It was a long day of straightening the kitchen, keeping food out, and putting it away before the heat of the July day spoiled it. But once again, my mother and sisters shared my workload and I was thankful.

Due to the July heat, Pastor Crawley performed the burial service late that afternoon. I stood between Ms. Adeline and Keane, both of them holding one of my hands. I felt like an intruder, and yet, I knew this was my place. I was not just a close neighbor anymore, but Keane's wife, or as the town now saw me, as his betrothed.

After the service, the evening was full of more food and even more guests. I could tell Ms. Adeline was exhausted and helped her to bathe after the last guest left at nearly ten that night. Once she was in a fresh nightgown, I brushed her long silver hair and tucked her into bed with a cup of chamomile tea.

Once again Keane took me home and whispered his gratitude for my help. I was beginning to see a kindness to his nature and it gave me great relief, for in only four days we would join four other couples in matrimony in the small country church. I sighed as I climbed wearily into bed. I was already a married woman, but it did not seem real to me.

I spent the next day with my mother and sisters as we drove into town to purchase material for my wedding dress. Celia had just finished hers, and it was lovely in a pale pink lawn with layers upon layers of white lace trim on the sleeves and skirt, along with a puffy pink bustle that sat atop layers of white lace trailing down to the floor. It was a beautiful gown and the first gown with a bustle that any of us girls had owned. But her dress, like mine, would still be practical enough to wear to a dinner or party and of course, Sunday church.

"What color would you like your dress to be, Georgie?" Mother asked me as we browsed the numerous bolts of fabrics.

I smiled and shook my head not having anything particular in mind. "Something light-weight preferably," I said, knowing how hot the church house was in July.

"That is our Georgie all right, nothing but practical," Valynn laughed. I smiled and took no offense to my sister. I was indeed very practical, and then I remembered what Keane had said the first day we met, that I was plain and backward. Suddenly I wanted a lovely dress like Celia's. I began to inspect the patterns and fabrics in earnest.

"What about this, Georgie?" Augusta held up a soft green lawn. I shrugged; it was a lovely color, but nothing extraordinary. Valynn found a silver-blue lawn; I nodded to keep that one in mind. Then I saw it, the perfect fabric for my wedding dress. It was a white lawn with tiny sprigs of blue flowers scattered faintly about.

"Oh how perfect, Georgie! It will bring out the blue of your eyes!" Genevieve said excitedly. We matched it with white eyelet and tiny white satin buttons. For a wedding gift, my sisters surprised me with a new pair of matching dress boots.

"Now let us hurry home, Girls, we only have three days to finish Georgie's dress and get both girls packed and ready to leave." Then with the realization that she was soon losing two of her babies, my mother gasped, tears filling her eyes as she gathered us close to her. Suddenly we all realized that within three days, two of the five of us girls would be forever leaving our home. Our joyful banter, evenings of music and reading, and whispering conversations with one another into the night, would all be forever changed. We all hugged one another and fought back our tears. The only one of us truly happy about the arrangement was sweet Celia, and nothing could dampen her glowing face. She was ready to be a bride. I found myself envious of her for the first time in my life.

We worked as a team cutting the fabric and sewing the three-piece dress. By late that evening, we had the skirt finished with its bustle and layers of eyelet down the back. I was more than pleased with the outcome and could not help but parade around the parlor in only my chemise and my skirt. My sisters smiled and laughed at my theatrics. I prayed for the next few days to go slowly so I could savor my time with them.

A knock at the door sent me hiding in the kitchen as I heard Valynn greet Keane and invite him in. I rushed up the back staircase. Augusta found me and helped me out of my frilly skirt and into my day dress. I had no time to redo my hair, so I left it hanging down my back loose and full of curls from our trip into town earlier. When I found Keane sitting in the parlor, my mother was visiting comfortably with him, and my sisters surrounded her on the sofa. He smiled when he looked up and saw me, and for a moment, I thought he might actually be happy to see me.

"Is Ms. Adeline well?" I asked, concerned and feeling a little guilty for not visiting that day, but there was so much to do before I moved to the Kenrick Farm.

"She is well. I came to see if you would like to take a walk with me?" he asked nervously.

I am certain my look was of surprise, but my mother quickly urged me on, nearly shoving us out the door, obviously pleased he wished to be alone with me. I blushed and asked him where he would like to walk. He suggested the back acreage that adjoined the Kenrick farm to my father's farm. We walked in silence for what seemed an eternity and finally he spoke.

"The house was finally quiet this afternoon," he said nervously.

I smiled. "I am certain that is welcome to you and Ms. Adeline after having a house full of people for days now."

He shrugged. "It was almost too quiet. We decided after dinner that we missed you, Mormor and I both," he said and I nearly choked. Keane Kenrick missed me?

I struggled with what to say. "Well, in just over two days you will be wishing I still lived at home. I will be around more than you wish, I am certain," I said, hating the tremor in my voice.

He shook his head no but said nothing. "Mormor doesn't cook as well as you either," he said with a grin. My stomach felt like butterflies as I took in his handsome grin; it irritated me to no end that he could make me feel like this. Perhaps I liked him better when he was cross with me?

"Is there anything that needs to be moved before the wedding? I would be happy to move it on over to the farmhouse," he said, staring out across the wheat fields.

"Not yet. I haven't finished packing. My mother took me into town this morning to buy fabric for my wedding dress. My sisters and I have been busy sewing all day. I just hope we finish it in time," I said softly.

"I am glad you're getting a new dress, Georgiana, you deserve it," he said, making me raise an eyebrow in question. I wanted to bring up his words just days ago about the money he had wanted to borrow to buy me out, and how he said I needed a few new dresses, but I remained quiet, knowing I hadn't yet forgiven him in my heart. I would need to try harder.

When he walked me back home, he took my hand in his and lightly kissed my knuckles. I could hardly breathe as I turned to go inside, knowing my sisters all spied from the windows above us.

"So what did he say tonight? Why did he want to walk with you?" Celia questioned once we were alone in our room.

I shrugged. "We didn't really speak about anything, but he said that Ms. Adeline and he both missed me," I said, still in shock.

Celia clapped her hands and bounced on her knees upon her bed. "I told you God heard me, and perhaps Valynn, too," she giggled.

As I lay in bed and tried to fall asleep, I wondered what Keane was doing at that very moment; if he ever thought of me when he lay down to sleep, or if it was still Melody's face he dreamed of.

The next day after chores, we resumed the sewing of my wedding dress. Much to my delight, it was finished by tea that afternoon. Eleanor Bentley and Millicent Smythe, the other two brides, came out to surprise us. We all sat in the parlor and visited while we embroidered our wedding handkerchiefs with our new initials. I used a light blue to match the small flowers on my dress and was quite pleased as Eleanor, my best friend, and Millie bragged on how lovely my wedding dress was. It was indeed the prettiest dress I had ever owned.

"You must wear a corset, Georgie, at least on your wedding day. I, myself, have taken to wearing them every day," Eleanor bragged. I frowned. I hated corsets and my figure was thin enough.

"Yes, you must, Georgie; it will give you curves and lift up your assets, or at least make it look as if you have assets," Valynn said, making us all giggle.

"I do not care to look as if I have assets," I laughed. "This marriage to Keane is for the farm only. He has made that quite clear," I said with a hint of regret.

"Oh Georgie, I am so sorry. I wanted so much more for you. But the Kenrick farm is beautiful. You will have the nicest home of us all," Eleanor said, hugging me close. I wanted no pity, and I was beginning to wonder if a farm could indeed make up for a loveless marriage?

"But you can always change his mind, Georgie dear, just play up your feminine wiles," Valynn said. I gasped, wondering how my innocent sixteen-year-old sister knew of such things.

"Valynn is right, Georgie; you will be alone in his house, wear a sweet perfume, leave your stockings and chemises lying about where he can see them, or on the clothesline. I have heard women say there are things you can do to entice men to notice you," Millie said sweetly.

I laughed and shook my head no. "I do not wish to entice Keane Kenrick. And you forget, Mrs. Kenrick will still be living with us. Do not worry for me; I will be happy once I own my beloved farm." I changed the subject now to ask Eleanor where they were going on their wedding trip, knowing she would now monopolize the conversation. And to my relief, she did.

CHAPTER THREE

After supper on the eve of my wedding, despite my having numerous things left to do before the next day, I walked across the fields to the Kenrick farm and found Ms. Adeline sitting on her front porch swing and hugged her warmly as I greeted her.

"I have your room all ready, my dear, although I was quite upset that Keane insisted you both wanted separate rooms. It was never heard of in my day. We women did our duties just as we were expected to. How will I ever have great grandchildren at this rate?" she asked, shaking her head at me.

I shrugged and looked away embarrassed. "I cannot promise you ever will, Ms. Adeline," I said just above a whisper. My heart ached at the thought of never having children of my own, but I would force myself to be content owning the farm. I had to.

"It is Keane, I know it is. You are so tender hearted; you would give into him if he wanted. I do not blame you, Georgie. Perhaps after his heart heals, he will come around," she said wistfully.

I shrugged again. "Perhaps," I whispered.

"I have seen a change in his actions toward you already, and it has only been six days. It was his idea to ride over last night, you know?" she said smiling.

I smiled and thanked her for sharing that with me. Our quiet walk the night before meant so much more to me now. I heard the back door slam and boots stomp through the house as Keane called for his Mormor.

"Out here, Keane," I called in return. He flung open the front screen door, and I knew in an instant, the old, cross Keane had returned.

"Keane, whatever is the matter?" Ms. Adeline asked, perturbed by his actions.

He lifted a telegram in his hand and tears filled his eyes, but they would not fall in front of us, I was certain, for he was much too angry. "This is what has become of your meddling, Mormor. Melody is now marrying Eitan," he said angrily. My heart felt as if an arrow had pierced it.

"Eitan, your brother?" she asked in shock.

"Yes, Eitan, my younger brother. And now, when I visit my family, I will be forced to see her and their babies when they have them, and I will be forced to watch them together and merely wish them well," he said with a broken voice. I covered my face with my hands, hurting for Keane and for myself, for I now saw the depths of his love for Melody.

"It is not my fault she marries Eitan, and so ridiculously soon; your parents should never have allowed it, knowing how you felt about her," Ms. Adeline insisted firmly. "And the girl herself, that is very vindictive of her. If she loved you so much, she shouldn't wish to be tied to your family knowing she would see you at every gathering," Ms. Adeline continued.

I stood to leave, excusing myself quietly. As I reached the front walk I heard Keane softly say, "Henry can see you home tonight."

I stopped but never turned to look at him. So he would not take me home. Well, I didn't need him anyway. "I can see myself home," I said, rushing away. He did not follow, and I was

38

thankful, for I could not help but cry, my heart aching for the hurt Keane felt, and in return, causing me.

My mother and Genevieve were finishing the baking for the wedding banquet on the morrow, my wedding banquet. I could only wonder if my groom would even show up. Then I realized it was too late. I was already married to this man and tomorrow's ceremony was simply for the town. The deed was already done. I was stuck in this farce of a marriage. I rushed away not able to speak to them and shut myself in my room. I would wake tomorrow with swollen eyes and splotchy skin, but I did not care. What had possessed me to think I had a right to own half of the Kenrick Farm? Why hadn't I simply given up my right of the farm to Keane? My heart ached, but I knew why I had made my choice. I needed a future. I needed a husband. If I did not marry Keane, then Celia, Valynn, Genevieve and Augusta would never have a chance to marry. Despite my insistence, Ms. Adeline would not give Keane the farm any other way. My heart ached as I continued to weep and pray for Keane, for Ms. Adeline, for myself, and even for Eitan and Melody.

The next morning found me where this story began....I was sitting in the church, on the front pew where Pastor Crawley had instructed us to wait while he spoke privately in the back room with the grooms. I wondered what sort of lecture the men were receiving. We brides had to sit through an hour sermon from the good Pastor's wife about loving, respecting, and obeying our husbands, and about giving ourselves freely in body to them. If I could have crawled under the pew, I would have. I had already endured my mother's birds and bees lecture the day before. While I was quite appalled, Celia had prolonged the discussion with questions, much to my mortification.

"Keane is here," I heard a small voice whisper and turned to see my youngest sister Augusta kneeling behind me, so that she was not seen. I thanked her for the useful information and ordered her back outside where the now arriving guests were mingling until they were let inside the church house. I had to admit a little surprise that he had shown up.

I heard boots shuffling across the floor, and Celia squeezed my hand warmly. "John looks so handsome today," she said, beaming with pride. Out of the corner of my eye I saw Keane, handsomely dressed in a dark blue shirt and white bow tie. It only made him look devastatingly handsome, I thought, as he found his way to the aisle across from us. I marveled at how fast Ms. Adeline could have purchased such a shirt after telling her the colors of my dress. But I could no longer think of such things as Keane's dark scowl met my hopeful gaze. Instead, I turned to face forward as the music began and the entire town and families of those being wed filed in and took their seats.

I felt near to faint, silently cursing the corset I had been talked into wearing. While it did accentuate my assets as my friends and sisters had ensured, I was suffering in pain. It wasn't as if Keane would even take notice, and now I had lost all ability to breathe due to the fact that there was no air circulating in the small church. How could women wear these every day? I marveled at how Eleanor and the other brides seemed so cool and calm, even excited, and they were all wearing corsets. I closed my eyes against my tears and misery and wondered how it would feel to be marrying a man who loved me, who wanted me with his entire being. My heart was so broken I could not even imagine such a love.

Pastor Crawley had everyone rise and opened the service with a beautiful prayer and then called the first couple forward, Eleanor and Matthias. I breathed a little easier knowing I had at least twenty minutes until he called the next couple forward. As I listened to my best friend pledge her life to Matthias, I had to dry a few tears. Eleanor was nineteen, just a few months younger than I, and we had both feared being spinsters. But luckily for Eleanor, Matthias Stein had taken notice of her six months ago. I was truly happy for Eleanor and was determined to tamp down any jealousy, for I was never a jealous person, until I met Keane Kenrick. Somehow he brought out the worst in me.

As Pastor Crawley announced Eleanor and Matthias man and wife, everyone stood and clapped in congratulatory fashion. Eleanor glowed with happiness. There was no mistaking the look of deep devotion in Matthias's eyes as he escorted his new bride to the aisle reserved just behind me. I discretely turned and clasped her hand in mine and smiled, "You look beautiful, Eleanor!" I whispered.

She squeezed my hand in hers. "You are next," she whispered. I quickly turned back around, praying another couple would be called, anyone but Keane and me. I wrung my handkerchief nervously. Would Keane and I be called next? His eyes met mine. His face was pale. He quickly looked straight ahead as if he were being sentenced to death.

"Would Drew Weston and Millicent Smythe please join me?" Pastor Crawley called. I could not help but let out a loud sigh of relief, causing Celia to blush and give me a most stern look. I did not care. Everyone knew the story around my impending marriage; they all knew it was not a love match but an arranged marriage by Mr. and Mrs. Kenrick, Keane's grandparents. I looked behind me to the side several rows back to where my parents sat smiling. Keane's grandmother sat beside them with a wistful sort of look on her face. Didn't she know she was destroying two lives this day? She caught me watching her and simply nodded a silent encouraging nod. I gave her a weak smile and turned to watch as Millicent and Drew said their vows. Millie was Celia's age, just turning eighteen. She looked a little nervous but glowed in the same way Eleanor and Celia did. Drew looked completely smitten.

I soon heard the Pastor announce them man and wife. Celia grabbed my hand, knowing one of us was next. I prayed it was Celia and John. I caught a glimpse of Keane looking toward the back door as if he might run from the building. I prayed he wouldn't, and yet part of me wished he would.

"Would John Stein and Celia Andley please join me?" Pastor Crawley asked with a gentle smile. I hugged my sister warmly and watched her gracefully make her way to the front and join hands eagerly with her love. Celia was lovely in her pale pink dress and auburn hair. I could see John drinking in the sight of her with appreciation. I turned to see tears of joy on my parents' faces, so happy. Even my sisters all seemed teary eyed. I quickly reminded myself I was doing this for them. I loved them, each one.

But it was something I had to continually remind myself every second until Pastor Crawley announced John and Celia man and wife. I knew Keane and I were next. I dreaded the ceremony. Such a silly thing when we had wed the week before.

Eleanor squeezed my shoulders gently behind me. "I am praying for you, Georgie," she said. I could only nod lest I begin to cry. I heard my name being called and somehow my feet were walking toward the front, in my pretty new wedding boots. I had felt rather pretty in my frilly new dress. Mother and my sisters had cried when I had dressed that morning. Celia and Valynn had spent an hour curling my long dark blonde hair into intricate spiral curls that hung over one shoulder. My bouquet of fresh daisies and lilies tied with matching white eyelet and blue ribbons, complimented my dress and blue eyes. My eyes found my groom's as he reached for my hand. He did not squeeze it tenderly as I had hoped, and I knew he could feel me trembling with nerves.

Pastor Crawley smiled and began the service. Somehow I managed to say my vows when appropriate, but Keane's voice lacked the warmth and sincerity it had a week before beside his grandfather's bedside. As he slid a ring over my finger, I glimpsed down and saw that he had purchased me a new one. This one contained a small diamond in the center of the gold band. I looked up surprised, not expecting such an expensive gift, but he did not acknowledge me. I, too, slipped a simple gold band on his finger and gave him my pledge, though my voice revealed my nervousness and doubts.

The Pastor announced Keane could kiss me now, and I truly feared he wouldn't. I feared the utter humiliation of it, with everyone watching. I mourned the fact that I wasn't even lovely enough to kiss, but to my delight and surprise, his lips found mine. They lingered longer than when he had kissed me when we had married last week. I could not help but squeeze his hands in appreciation. He looked dazed or confused when our lips parted, but he quickly tucked my hand into his arm.

Since we were the last couple to wed, we led the other brides and grooms out to where the reception had been set up on the church lawn. Each couple had their own table that allowed people to stop and greet the newlyweds and to leave their gifts. Our table had been decorated by my sisters in a lovely white tablecloth and a bouquet of blue bonnets and daisies mixed with lilies in the center. Celia's table sat next to ours so that our family could share between the two of us.

Ms. Adeline came to sit on the other side of Keane as his family. "You have made us proud, my grandson," she said, kissing his cheek. He smiled weakly and hugged her tight, his tall and muscular stature so magnificent against her small and tiny person.

She hugged me close. "Georgie, you look radiant! Yours is the prettiest dress here," she exclaimed. I thanked her and blushed wondering if Keane found me attractive in the least. Pastor Crawley blessed the food, and Mother offered to bring us each a plate so that we could visit with our guests. I smiled and thanked her, knowing she read my mind. I was so nervous there was no way I could walk to the food lines, and this corset was poking deeply into my ribs. I doubted I could eat a bite.

The town folks all passed by us, hugging us, shaking hands, and wishing us well. Some left jars of canned vegetables and fruits; others crocheted doilies and quilts. I could see their generosity had some effect on Keane as he soon leaned over to me and asked if they were always so friendly and giving.

I smiled and nodded. "We are a close community," I whispered back, and he seemed completely in shock. Soon John and Matthias, along with Drew, came and took Keane from me to visit with the men. I breathed a sigh of relief as my sisters gathered around me. I hugged each of them, enjoying how happy they were this day. Celia was nearly floating on air with happiness; somehow it made this difficulty of mine worthwhile.

"I am just about to faint," I confessed quite seriously in her embrace. She giggled as I tried to discretely pull the corset out a little to breathe.

"Oh, Georgie, do leave it alone, you look stunning!" she insisted.

"Did I hear someone say 'Georgie'?" I turned as I heard an unfamiliar male voice.

At first I did not recognize the speaker, but soon I realized just who it was. "Robert Anderson?" I asked softly.

He smiled, and I knew for certain it was he, his young sixteen-year-old body now that of a grown man. "Little Georgie Andley!" he said, taking both of my hands in his and smiling brightly. I nodded and my heart nearly stopped. Was fate playing a cruel trick on me again?

"Well, you're not the little girl I nearly courted four years ago; you're a stunning woman now," he said, pleased with my appearance and causing me to blush.

"I cannot believe you are here; when did you arrive in town?" I asked, wishing it would have been a week ago; perhaps I hadn't waited for whom God had for me after all. The thought made my knees shake.

"Just now, in fact, Uncle Micah just pulled up for the reception. He picked me up at the train station and told me we were missing the weddings but would arrive for the luncheon," he said excitedly. I could not help but frown. Why hadn't he come sooner?

"He said it was a large wedding with four or five couples?" he continued, trying to make conversation.

I could not answer, so my sweet sister Valynn spoke up for me. "Yes, four couples," she answered cautiously.

"How nice," he said, looking around the church yard. He still had hold of my hands in his, and it was then that he felt the diamond on my new wedding band. His eyes met mine and I thought I saw a hint of disappointment. "And you, little Georgie, are one of the brides?" he asked softly, as realization sat in.

Suddenly warm hands were around my waist behind me, and I smelled his spicy scented cologne before I saw that my husband had decided to join me. "Yes, Georgiana is the loveliest bride here, and now, Mrs. Georgiana Kenrick. And you are?" Keane asked nicely, but I could hear a little agitation underlying in his voice, and I wondered what I had done to anger him now?

Robert gave me a weak smile and nodded. My heart ached; I had pined after Robert for nearly a year after he left. I was going to faint; I just knew it. When was the last time I had eaten? And did they have to have the reception in the middle of the hottest day in July?

"Excuse me, Keane, this is an old friend, Robert Anderson. He just arrived in town, just now. Robert, this is my husband, Keane Kenrick," I said, as if I could have willed Robert to have arrived earlier, a few weeks earlier. My eyes sought his and my heart ached to ask why he had stopped writing me four years ago. But I knew I could not and perhaps I would never know. Keane reached out and shook his hand civilly. Robert wished us well although his eyes held a little disappointment in them as he moved on to greet my parents.

I nearly collapsed; Keane's arms went up higher around me. "Georgiana, are you well?" he asked rather panicked. My eyes met his brilliant blue ones and then the world went black.

The next thing I heard were men's voices arguing in the distance, echoing as if in a well. I heard Celia's voice though it was quite muffled as I struggled to wake. I needed air desperately. "It is the first time she has worn a corset, Dr. Anderson. I fear I might have tied it too tightly," I heard her say. I tried to protest at her mentioning such a personal thing; surely Robert was not the new doctor coming to town.

Then I heard Keane's voice. "I am her husband, if anyone is taking off her unmentionables, it is I!" I felt hands unbuttoning my dress quickly and rolling me onto my side. Then, I felt a tugging at the back laces, and in an instant I could breathe. I gasped for air as the room whirled about me.

"It is all right, Georgie, you're all right," I heard Robert say.

"She doesn't like to be called Georgie," Keane said, rudely.

"Perhaps she just doesn't like you calling her Georgie, but she will always be Georgie to me," Robert insisted firmly. I had to wake; I had to stop this nonsense.

A cool rag washed over my face and chest. "Let me do that," I heard Keane insist. "She is my wife!" My stomach once again did little flutters as he called me his wife, although I doubted if I would have had his attention at all had Robert not been friendly towards me. As the room came into focus, I could see I was in the small backroom of the church lying across the Pastor's desk. Both Robert and Keane were hovering over me, and Celia was standing in the doorway.

"Oh thank heavens! Georgie, are you all right?" she asked, rushing to me.

I nodded as I took in Robert's set of brown eyes and Keane's dark blue ones. "I am sorry, but what happened?" I asked, trying to piece together the afternoon. All I could remember was Robert, his hands in mine, and then Keane coming over, his hands on my waist.

"You fainted, Georgie," Robert said with a smile. "Ms. Celia, could I ask you to bring your sister a glass of lemonade?" he asked sweetly. Keane frowned. I heard her rush away, and Keane's arms went behind me to help me sit up.

Robert leaned in close. "So, first time wearing a corset? And might I ask if you remembered to eat anything today?" he asked. I blushed and heard Keane curse as he heard Robert bring up something as personal as a corset.

"Do not worry; your secret is safe with me. I am assisting Dr. Childers in town; I am in my last year of medical school doing my internship here. And as your doctor, I insist you eat something," he said smiling warmly.

He wasn't as handsome or muscular as Keane, but he had such lovely manners and seemed just like the old Robert, so easy to talk to. I wondered again why he had stopped writing to me four years ago. Had he married? I assured him that I would eat. I looked down to see my assets still perched upward above the corset even though it had been loosened somewhat, with only my thin chemise protecting most of the top of me. My dress top was lying beside me on the desk. "Oh my goodness!" I squealed, covering myself with my arms, my cheeks flaming red. "Please turn around, both of you!" I demanded, quickly reaching for my top.

I felt warm hands on my shoulders. "Let me help you dress, Georgiana," Keane whispered near my ear, causing goose pimples to cover my body.

"I shall find *our Georgie* some nourishment," I heard Robert say, leaving the room. He had said *'our Georgie'*. How sweet and heart wrenching his sentiment was.

My hands trembled as I looked to Keane, who was trying to figure out my laces behind me. "I must admit I have never seen one of these," he chuckled nervously. "But I will be hanged if I let that friendly doctor do it." I suddenly realized he was jealous. My heart soared; I had hope for the first time that day.

Luckily Celia returned with the lemonade and ushered both men out of the room as she dressed me and forced me to eat. She helped straighten up my hair and retied the ribbon. Then, arm and arm we went back outside. The crowds were clearing off tables and preparing to go home. Pastor Crawley announced that there would be a barn dance at the Stein Farm the coming Saturday night in honor of the newly wedded couples, since two of their sons had wed that day. I smiled and looked to Keane, but his frown told me he might not agree to going.

I was pleased to see he had at least driven his buggy. My parents found me and asked Keane to come by for my things that evening. They would take Ms. Adeline on home to Kenrick Farms, and we could eat supper with them when we came to pick up my belongings. Keane smiled warmly and thanked them.

The other couples who had married with us gathered around as the photographer we had hired took each couple's photograph. Eleanor made us promise to come to dinner two weeks from the day. I looked to Keane first before agreeing, and he nodded with a weak smile. I was thrilled with the upcoming dance and dinner at Eleanor and Matthias's home. It would surely break up the monotony of farm life, especially now that I would have to live with a very cross husband.

On the drive home with our buggy loaded down with food and gifts, Keane asked softly, "Want to tell me who Robert is?" I looked up surprised and knew I was blushing.

"He is just as I said, an old friend. We were good friends. After he moved to the city, he wrote me a few times telling me about city life, and then he stopped writing. There is nothing more to tell," I said, staring out at the wheat fields.

"He seemed sweet on you," Keane said bluntly.

I had to turn my head and hide a smile. "He could be married for all we know. I think you mistook friendship for something more," I said softly.

He stopped the buggy. "I know when a man finds a woman beautiful. That new doctor finds you beautiful, Georgiana." His eyes were seriously searching mine.

I blushed and looked down at my lap. "He would be the first man then," I whispered.

"I doubt that. Anyone can see how pretty you are, especially today. Although you were pretty before you wore that contraption that made you look more like a woman than you should have," he said, angrily driving the team on.

So he had noticed the difference of the corset, I thought silently. "Well, at least Robert doesn't think I am plain and backward," I said, regretting it the moment I said it.

He stopped the team once more with a jerk. I scowled at being thrown forward, grasping the top of the buggy for support. "Who said you were plain and backward?" he demanded, as if it insulted him that someone should think such a thing.

My eyes filled with tears as they met his. "You did, the day we met."

Once we were home, I went up to the room that was now to be mine and found the extra dress I had left there. I desperately needed to bathe the perspiration off me. I was still feeling hot and woozy from too much sun and corset. I quickly changed, barely getting out of the contraption as Keane called it, and I stuffed it into an empty drawer, telling myself I would only use it in case of a marital emergency. I put on my clean dress, gathered soap and towels, and decided to sneak down to the creek for a swim and bath. Henry and Keane were taking care of the animals, and I told Ms. Adeline where I was going so no one would worry.

After being in so many crowds over the last week, I enjoyed my solitary trek to the back of the property. My sisters and I had discovered the creek and deep swimming hole when we were young and spent many a hot afternoon on its banks. Once I stripped down to my chemise, I ran and jumped off the bank into the deep. Coming up gasping for air with my hair plastered to my face, I smiled as my body temperature decreased rapidly. It was lovely swimming around in the deep, listening to the wind rushing through the tall wheat and to the gurgling and rushing of the creek itself. My thoughts went to Robert, and once again I wondered if he had married? Had I been too hasty agreeing to this farm and marriage with Keane? Did he feel we were out of God's will? Is that why he fought me so hard each day? What if God had Robert for me all along and I had missed his will for my life? But even now, I could not release the thoughts of being part owner of Kenrick Farms. I loved the farm and Ms. Adeline. It felt like a second home to me, or at least it had until Keane had arrived.

"May I join you?" I heard a man ask.

I screamed as I whirled around to see Keane with a handsome smirk on his face. "What are you doing here? Of course, I mind. I am not decent!" I yelled back at him.

He chuckled out loud. "Mormor told me where you had gone. She didn't feel it was safe for you to be alone. I must agree," he said, making himself at home taking off his work boots on the bank.

"I have been coming here for fifteen years and never have I met with danger. I do not need a chaperone," I insisted.

"I am certain you did not come alone," he said, knowing my family would never have allowed it, and my cheeks flamed red, knowing he was right. We always had to go in two's. "And surely you would not make me sit in the hot sun and wither away with this cool water just waiting to refresh me," he teased. I frowned. There went my perfect afternoon alone. "I will not come near you. You have my word. I am in love with another, remember?" he asked.

If he had been anywhere close, I would have slapped him. "How could I forget, and thank you for bringing up such a subject on our wedding day," I smarted off. I swam away towards the opposite side and screamed again as the water splashed close behind me, and I caught a glimpse of skin under the water. Keane was swimming in his drawers.

"That does feel good!" he said, shaking the water from his blondish-brown hair. He wore no shirt, and I blushed as I turned away. "We should do this each evening. It is rather relaxing," he said, as he floated on his back.

"The water might be too cool in the evening, but late afternoon before choring might be nice," I said, still facing the other direction.

"Naw, I say right after supper, before we go to bed. That upstairs is stifling hot. I may enclose the back porch; make it a sleeping porch. What do you think?" he asked.

I turned; shocked he had asked my opinion on something. "That would be nice," I said softly. I swam to shore and reached out for the scented soap, then swam back out to the far side and began to wash my hair. I didn't hear Keane making any splashes and quickly turned to find him watching me, the oddest look on his face. I turned away and nearly growled angrily. I just wanted to swim, alone.

"You know, I am sorry for what I said that day; I never thought you would overhear it. And it isn't true. You are far from plain and never backward," he said tenderly.

I did not turn around but thought silently, 'I am only backward around you and I wonder why'? "You do not have to lie to me, Keane; you are free to think whatever you desire," I said sarcastically.

"I never lie, Georgiana. Sometimes I am cruelly blunt, but that day I was so hurt and angry, I did lie to my grandmother. I was desperate and thought if she would only give Melody a chance, she would like her as much as you. I thought if I said you were plain and convinced her you wouldn't please me, she would give up on her demands to make us marry. But regardless of why I did it, I did it. I lied. I find you very lovely," he said breathlessly.

I ignored him and sank down deeper into the water, rinsing my hair and praying when I went to the top of the water he would be gone. I had my eyes open and looked at the colors of the stones and small fish trying to nibble on my drawers. I loved it here. If only Celia and Valynn had joined me. I began to mentally recite The Lord's Prayer to calm myself.

All of a sudden something yanked on my hair and pulled me to the surface. Keane's frightened face met my angry one. "Can you breathe?" he asked, slapping me hard on the back.

I began to choke and he held me close. "I am not drowning, you idiot!" I screamed at him, but I might as well have slapped him the way he looked.

"Yes, you were drowning! Were you doing it on purpose? I saw the bubbles and you never came up," he argued, still holding me. The frightened look in his eyes told me he had been sincere. I rubbed my throbbing head that now smarted from his yanking my hair to pull me to the surface. "I am sorry, Georgiana; I truly thought you were drowning," he said embarrassed.

"Why would I drown myself on purpose?" I asked, wincing in pain. The look on his face was too much. Suddenly, I began to laugh. I do not know why. My head throbbed like the dickens and I was so mad at him, at least I wanted to be mad at him. He began to laugh, too. When I could finally speak, I informed him. "If you see bubbles, it means I am breathing. When the bubbles stop, that is when I need saving," I chuckled.

He nodded, still embarrassed. "Right, I will remember that next time. How did you stay down there so long anyway?" he asked, as if it amazed him.

I shrugged and swam away from him, suddenly uncomfortable with his closeness. "I suppose with four sisters, you just find places to be alone when you can. I would sit underneath the water, hold my breath, and count or recite scripture, pushing myself farther and longer each time," I said, stopping to search for my soap. "Well, that bar is gone," I said with a sigh.

Keane just shook his head. "Better a bar of soap than my wife," he said and trudged up to the shore. My stomach fluttered at the small fact that I was at least more important to him than the soap.

I was apprehensive when we drove the wagon to my parent's home. I wanted the Kenrick Farm, but at the same time I was already feeling a little homesick. Tonight I would go to sleep in a new bed, in a new room, in a new house. I would miss Celia; we had shared a room since her birth. Keane had been quiet the rest of the afternoon, and now, I longed for the noise of home and my four sisters. I feared I might beg my parents to let me stay at home once I saw them.

"Your family has a nice farm," I heard and looked over to see Keane with a gentle smile on his face. I nodded. I had always loved our place. The house was not as grand as the Kenrick home, but it was cozy and the love it held inside its walls had made it the grandest house to me. My sisters gathered around us in a swarm, each making doe eyes at my handsome husband. I had to giggle.

I found Mother in the kitchen as Father took Keane out to see a new horse in the barn. "Are you feeling better, my love? You still look quite pale," my mother asked, kissing my cheek.

"I am better, thank you," I said, hugging her warmly. "Are John and Celia coming?" I asked, hopeful.

Mother smiled and shook her head. "No, they came right after the reception; Celia said she did not want to spend her honeymoon with us," she said with a smile.

I blushed. "When do they leave for the Falls?" I asked, knowing that is where they planned to take their wedding trip.

"Monday morning. They will be gone for two weeks and return just in time to help with the Stein's harvest," she said, handing me the bread to put on the table.

"Will Keane take you to the dance at the Stein's Saturday night?" Valynn asked excitedly.

"Of course he will, Valynn for they are one of the married couples. They must attend," Mother said but then paused when she looked at my worried face.

I looked her in the eyes; mine now filling with tears. "I do not expect him to," I whispered, remembering the scowl he had when it was announced. "The sooner everyone remembers this marriage is for the farm only, the better off I will be," I said rather spitefully.

Mother hugged me close. "Give him time, Georgie. We will pray he comes around. I will have your father speak to him about the dance. You must attend, even if your marriage is in name only. Surely he isn't opposed to dancing?" she said tenderly.

"He is opposed to anything that involves me," I said, drying my tears.

"I could beat the thunder out of him for you if you'd like," Valynn said, her eyes now full of tears as well.

"I will help her! No one treats our Georgie like this," Genevieve said stomping her foot.

I had to laugh, and soon my sisters laughed with me. "I hope you will all choose your husbands wisely. Choose for love. That is the only reason I am doing this. It is for you. I love the farm but have moments when I am certain it is not enough to keep me there. But each of you is reason enough," I said smiling. They all hugged me closely and I cherished their loving embraces.

Dinner was wonderful. I found myself wishing the night never had to end. But my trunks were loaded and ready to go. I hugged each of my sisters goodbye, but my mother I clung to. "We will see you at the dance Saturday night if not before," I heard my father say.

Keane looked surprised. I released my mother and looked to him. "I am not much of a dancer," he said firmly.

My father raised his chin higher. "Well, Georgie is, and she can teach you, but the Stein's expect to see you there, and I will as well," Father said and wished us a goodnight. Keane didn't look happy, but I was truly overjoyed. No matter what the next few days brought, I had something to look forward to.

We drove home as the sun set; I smiled as I looked out over our wheat and the pink and purple sunset. "It is beautiful, isn't it?" I asked Keane without thinking.

"Yes it is. It is why I could never live in town," he said with a gentle smile.

I smiled in return and nodded. "I agree. Farm life is in my blood. I would not be happy in town," I said wistfully. Keane looked deep in thought, so I did not wish to interrupt him.

Once we arrived at the farmhouse, I carried in the plate of food my mother had sent Ms. Adeline and made her a cup of chamomile tea. After Henry and Keane carried my trunks upstairs to my room, they stopped to enjoy a piece of left over wedding cake with a cup of coffee. Ms. Adeline excused herself to her room for the night even though it was earlier than usual for her, but I knew she was still hoping that something romantic would happen between Keane and me with this being our official wedding night.

I cleaned the kitchen and then went to my room to begin unpacking my belongings. I was tired, but restless. I did not want to admit that I wished for more on my wedding night, like perhaps a wedding trip like the other brides were taking, but a part of me longed for those things. After I washed at the basin in my room and put on my summer nightgown, I sat upon my new bed and took out my Bible. I opened to Isaiah 41:10, "Fear thou not; for I am with thee; be not dismayed; For I am thy God; I will strengthen thee; yea I will help thee; yea I will uphold thee with the right hand of my righteousness." Tears filled my eyes. I had long leaned upon these promises. "I am not alone," I whispered as I dimmed my light. It wasn't even fully dark yet, and on my wedding night, I lay alone. "I am not alone," I whispered once again. I heard footsteps on the stairs and I held my breath. They paused before my door, and I waited, but then I heard Keane open his bedroom door, and then it shut. I willed my tears away as sleep finally overtook me.

CHAPTER FOUR

Rising early the next morning, I gathered the eggs and then did the milking. I was busy making breakfast when Ms. Adeline greeted me in her sleeping robe. "This smells wonderful, Georgie, but you are up so early," she said, taking a seat at the kitchen table with her Bible.

I was frying bacon and making cinnamon flapjacks as Keane came into the kitchen. "I will do the milking and be back for breakfast," he said with a frown.

"I have already done the milking and gathered the eggs," I said without looking to him.

"You did?" he asked, shocked. I nodded. "Why?" he asked.

I turned with a frown. "I am sorry; I am used to doing those things at home. I suppose I will need to know what is expected of me now," I said nervously.

"I guess I hadn't thought much about it yet. But I thank you for your help," he said, sitting down with his grandmother.

"Would you like coffee?" I asked.

"I can get it," he said, jumping to his feet. So I let him. "Would you like a cup?" he asked. I smiled and thanked him. "It smells wonderful," he complimented. I set the platter of flapjacks on the table and reached for the bacon.

"Ms. Adeline, is your syrup in the cellar?" I asked.

"Yes, dear, along with the butter in the cool room of the well house," she said smiling.

I nodded, but Keane jumped to his feet. "Let me at least get those things for you. I need to call Henry in to eat anyway," he said, rushing to help me.

"Thank you," I said softly in shock.

"Bring your coffee and sit with me," Ms. Adeline urged. I did as she asked, and within a few moments Keane and Henry returned with the butter and maple syrup. "Georgie, now that you are family here, we hold hands at prayer time," Ms. Adeline said, smiling. I nodded and took her hand and hesitantly took Keane's as he and Henry took hands. I had helped with breakfast at Kenrick Farms before, and Ms. Adeline and Jorik had never held hands as they prayed at breakfast before. She said a lovely prayer, and then we ate breakfast as Henry and Keane planned their day.

"Can I just say how happy I am you are here now, Georgie? These are the best flapjacks I have ever had," Henry said, smiling and taking three more off the stack. I smiled, pleased that at least I could make someone happy.

"Georgie is an excellent cook," Ms. Adeline agreed.

Keane nodded. "That she is," he said softly, not looking at me. After another helping of flapjacks, Keane pushed his plate back and sighed. "You know, my original plans in coming to Kenrick Farms was to start my horse breeding business. Of course, I will continue planting and farming, but my dream has always been to start my own stables here. I want to breed and raise Percheron horses. They are just new to the country; I saw one last year at the state fair. Earlier this spring, I spent my savings and bought one of the stud horses that came off the ship from France. I call him Gaspard. I wanted to wait and see how the farm was set up before I sent for him. My dream is to bring him here before the end of the year and start breeding. Henry, do you know of any place I could get a Percheron or Arabian mare?" Keane asked deep in thought.

Ms. Adeline and I looked to one another, surprised. So, sometime soon, Kenrick Farms would also be a stable? Keane continued to tell us everything he knew of the breed and how he wanted to design the stables. The men left to look at the fields, and I went to clean the kitchen.

"I can do this, dear. You did cook after all," Ms. Adeline said, taking over.

It was her house, and I was unsure of what my role was here. I nodded and thanked her. "I am going to work in the garden before the heat sets in if you do not mind. It looks as if there is a large crop of green beans ready to pick," I said, taking off my kitchen apron and tying a kerchief over my hair.

"Yes, of course. You're such a help to me, Georgie. There may be enough to start our canning even," she said smiling. I nodded and grabbed the cloth bags on the bag porch that women used to gather fruits and vegetables.

First, I hauled bucket after bucket of water from the well and gave everything in the garden a good soaking. Then, I began to pick the beans that had nearly been left too long. After both the cloth bags were full, I dumped them into a metal tub to wash later and went back for more beans.

Ms. Adeline came out, covered her lap with an old towel and began to snap the beans I had picked. We worked together for nearly two hours then set about cooking the beans to preserve them. I put a pan of the green beans on the back of the stove, cut up a small onion, and added some ham and new potatoes. It would make an easy dinner with cornbread while we were working canning the beans. The small kitchen was hot and more than once I dreamt of going to the creek to swim.

By one o'clock we had ten quarts of green beans put up and dinner was ready for Henry and Keane. Ms. Adeline cut up lemon for our tea, and I rang the dinner bell, calling the men inside.

"It is like an oven in here," Keane said, smiling as he observed our morning's work.

Ms. Adeline shooed him into the formal dining room. "We will eat in there for dinner. Georgie has been canning up a storm in here," she said smiling. I carried the meal into the dining room and Keane surprised me bringing in the butter and cornbread. I thanked him and once again, we all held hands while Ms. Adeline blessed the meal.

"Umm, this is wonderful," Henry bragged again. I blushed, for it was such a simple meal, but I was happy everyone seemed to enjoy it.

"It would make a nice day for a swim," I heard Keane say. I blushed; I wasn't for certain why.

"I agree, Keane. Perhaps we should all retire for a few hours until the sun goes down a little," Ms. Adeline said, smiling.

"I am all for it," Henry said.

"You swim, Ms. Adeline?" I asked, surprised.

She smiled. "I wade. And please, Georgie, you are family now. I am Mormor," she said, insisting I use the Swedish name of grandmother just as Keane did.

I smiled at the thought of her wading in the creek. My cheeks burned as I wondered what I would swim in, and if it would be appropriate in front of Henry. It was bad enough that Keane had interrupted my time the day before. "My sisters might be there. Perhaps I should go first to make sure they are decent," I said embarrassed.

"No need. I intend to take you to our swimming hole. It is a little further out, but it is lovely. Jorik and I haven't been down there for a year or two, but I am certain it is still there," she said excitedly.

"It is for a fact. That is where I bathe all summer," Henry said casually, making me blush. Keane burst into laughter, and I looked up surprised.

"I think you both are embarrassing my wife," he said, giving me a wink that made my stomach summersault.

"Well, we will not be bathing together for heaven's sake, just soaking our feet in the water. I intend to nap in the shade. Henry can take me in the buggy; I doubt I will last as long in the heat at my age," Ms. Adeline said quickly.

An hour later we followed the buggy on horseback to the most beautiful swimming hole I had ever seen. It put our Andley swimming hole to shame. "Oh, it is gorgeous!" I called out to Ms. Adeline as Keane helped me down from the horse.

"Are you going to swim in that dress?" he asked softly with a smirk.

"Yes, thank you, I am," I said, leaving him and helping Henry take out the large watermelon I had brought to soak in the cold stream.

Keane carried several old quilts as well as jugs of well water to set them in the cold creek. "Look, there is a rope hanging from the tree. How old is the rope, Mormor?" Keane asked intrigued.

"About five years, or perhaps ten, I think. Henry, do you remember when you put that up there?" she asked, settling onto a quilt in the shade.

"Not rightly sure, Ms. Addie. But go on, you young whipper-snapper and test it out," the older man encouraged Keane.

I laughed and dared to hope it snapped as Keane swung off on it. But it proved to be strong, and soon he was calling for me to swing with him. I shook my head no and daintily dangled my legs in the water under my long skirts. I would most likely drown if I tried swimming in so many garments. "Come on now; are you afraid?" he taunted.

I raised my head high. "No, I am not afraid, but I am not appropriately attired to do so," I said, teasing him back. He had a mischievous smile, and I had to laugh at his light mood; he could actually be enjoyable when he wanted. Henry went next, and for the next hour the men took turns running on the bank and swinging down to the creek with a splash.

After I tired of sitting in one place with my feet perched in the water, I joined Ms. Adeline on a quilt and lay back in the shade. "Well, Henry, I do believe I am done in. Let's leave these youngsters here, and you can take me home," she said, standing and taking up the book she had brought along. I blushed, as I knew she hoped we would spend time together, and in truth, I was dying to swim. My head and arms were quite hot and dangling my feet under a heavy skirt had not been very gratifying.

Keane helped his mormor into the buggy and kissed her cheek. "All right now, we are alone; do not tell me you were content with just your feet in the water," Keane said teasingly. I smiled, but my cheeks felt very warm. "I will turn around and you call

64

to me when you're in the water," he said, standing on the creek bank and turning his back to me.

I jumped up and slid off my heavy skirt down to my drawers and chemise. Then I climbed up the steep bank to where the rope hung. "I will show you I am not afraid. You are in love with a city girl, but you will learn soon enough, never dare a farm girl," I said, laughing as I grabbed ahold of the rope. He turned around laughing as I swung high off the bank and dropped just above the water with a loud squeal. He soon joined me taking turns swinging and dropping into the water.

A few hours later as we rode back to the house, I realized how much I had enjoyed the afternoon with Keane. We might not ever love one another, but perhaps we could be friends.

That evening I baked a chicken with vegetables and made a fresh strawberry pie. After dessert we sat on the porch swing watching the sunset. Mormor, as I now called her, once again excused herself to her room.

"I have been thinking about how to divide up the chores," I heard Keane say softly. I nodded and looked to him waiting. "In just a few weeks I will be quite busy with harvesting the wheat, but until then, I will gather the eggs and do both milkings, morning and evenings. You work very hard, Georgiana, perhaps too hard. I want you to take time to spend with Mormor or with sewing. I know I will rely on you more when harvest comes, but for the next couple of weeks, let me be of some help to you," he said tenderly.

I nodded and thanked him. "I had fun today, Keane, thank you," I whispered softly, standing to go to bed.

"Are you tired?" he asked suddenly. I shrugged. "I wouldn't mind your company for a bit longer and another piece of your strawberry pie," he said teasing. I blushed and pretended to slap his shoulder playfully and went back to get him another piece of pie and cup of coffee. My heart sang with the hope that perhaps he could think of me as a friend as well.

The next morning Mormor and I set to making strawberry preserves. Her garden was large enough to feed two families, but I felt confident over the next month we would have a cellar full of wonderful foods preserved, and it was nice to have extra on hand to take to those who were sick or down on their luck.

For dinner I used left over chicken and made chicken salad sandwiches, to Henry's delight. Keane helped me carry down the jars of preserves to the cellar and mocked the way I arranged fruits on one side alphabetically and vegetables on another.

"I need to go into town to purchase screen for the back porch; would you like to ride along?" he asked, hopeful.

Mormor nodded for me to go. "I wouldn't mind a nap myself," she said, handing me a small list of things to get at the mercantile.

The top item on the list was in a different penmanship and it said, "Fabric for Georgiana a dress." I laughed and then said, "I did not write this," as Keane helped me into the covered buggy.

He smiled. "No, I did. You need some practical summer dresses. And maybe some sort of swimming get-up," he winked at me, and I shook my head.

"I do not want pretty dresses to work in the garden and get dirty," I insisted.

"Your dresses look like they came from Mormor's day. Dirty or not, you need a few new ones. I insist," he said tenderly. I thanked him and was suddenly excited to look at the fabrics again.

"Georgie, how are you doing?" I heard and turned straight into Robert Anderson.

"Oh, I am sorry!" I said, taking a step back, and yet he stepped forward.

"Forgive me; I was across the street when I saw you walk in. Are you feeling better, I hope?" he asked warmly.

I blushed at the remembrance of my fainting on my wedding day. "Yes, much better thank you," I said nervously.

"Will you be going to the dance tomorrow evening?" he asked, hopeful. My heart raced as I nodded. "Good, then will you save me a dance?" he asked, just as Keane found me.

Keane greeted Robert, but not warmly. His hand went to the small of my back possessively. I nodded to Robert that I would save him a dance, and thankfully he left the store.

"Where are your fabrics?" Keane asked.

"Oh, Mrs. Larkin is cutting them for me in the back," I stumbled.

"Good, how many did you get?" he asked.

I released a breath I didn't realize I had been holding and smiled. "Four," I answered.

"Only four?" he asked, disappointed.

I laughed. "Four is plenty," I assured him.

"For now perhaps," he said, leading me to the counter. As Keane loaded the buggy with the supplies, I bid Mrs. Larkin a good day and saw Robert wave from the doctor's office across the street. I waved and blushed and quickly took Keane's hand as he helped me into the buggy. And for some odd reason as we went to drive away, Keane took my hand and held it tightly, perhaps possessively, and merely for Robert's eyes to see. But I enjoyed it just the same.

When we returned home, I quickly went up to my room and lay out the printed fabrics I had purchased. I wished I had more time to make a dress for the dance, but I knew nothing would compare to the loveliness of my wedding dress; I would of course wear it to the dance. I had chosen the silver-blue material Valynn had shown me the week before, and the sage green lawn that Augusta had chosen. I also chose a soft yellow material with tiny white polka dots and a peach material with small white stripes.

A knock sounded at the door, and I opened it to find Keane. "Would you like to go for a swim? Henry went into town to visit his brother, and Mormor is still resting," he said.

I looked at the material and sighed. The upstairs was getting quite hot; perhaps I could sew in the evenings. "I suppose it is all right," I said with a smile. He smiled in return. I quickly put a roast beef and potatoes and carrots in the oven and followed him out to the barn. He helped me onto a horse and then mounted his own.

We raced through the fields with him winning, of course, due to my uncertainty of my own ability to ride. Again he waited while I undressed to my underthings and swung off the rope into the water before joining me. We swam for over an hour until dark clouds began to roll in.

"About the dance, Keane, can you dance?" I asked, concerned. I knew he seemed very hesitant to go and thought perhaps he couldn't dance well. He shrugged. "I can tell you do not want to go," I stated bluntly. He shrugged again. "Can you tell me why you do not want to go?" I asked, irritated with his silent shrugs.

He sighed. "I guess because it will remind me of Melody. We met at a dance, and I proposed at a dance," he said, sighing, and then looking away.

I sighed, too. I had been looking forward to the dance all week. But to know it would bring Keane pain bothered me. "You do not have to go; I am certain my father would take me," I said tenderly, as we rode back towards home.

"I am expected to be there. Who knows, maybe I will enjoy it," he said, giving me a weak smile that turned my stomach into butterflies. "Besides, Dr. Anderson would be thrilled if I didn't show up; he would most likely take all your dances. Can't let that happen," he chuckled. My heart raced. He was jealous, but how? When he loved Melody so much? I simply shook my head and blushed. I hated to admit it, but I was very confused by Keane's behavior.

A nice rain blew in. I relished the coolness it brought into my room upstairs where, after dinner, I worked, sewing the first of my new dresses. A knock sounded at my door, and I opened it to find Keane standing there smiling. "Mormor said if you would bring your material downstairs, she would help you in the parlor."

I smiled. "Surely you would both like a little time alone without me?" I replied, gathering up my things.

Keane took the sewing basket from me and smiled. "Not really," he said as we headed downstairs.

I didn't mind; it helped me with the loneliness that seemed to plague me come nighttime. "Are you certain you want to help me with my sewing, Mormor?" I asked her.

She smiled and nodded. "Actually, Georgie, I will pin your pattern on if you will play us a tune on the piano. It has been far too long since this house had any music in it. My fingers just aren't the same as they used to be. I would enjoy a cup of tea and hearing you play," she said smiling.

I kissed her cheek and asked Keane if he would like tea or coffee. Within minutes I had returned with them each a cup of tea and a plate of rhubarb pie. "What would you like to hear?" I asked, taking my place at the piano.

"Oh, anything you like, my dear," Mormor said.

"This sure is good pie, Georgiana," Keane said smiling. I thanked him and turned to play, choosing a piece from Mozart and then a few hymns. Outside there was gentle thunder reverberating, and in Mormor's cozy parlor with the lamps all lit, playing the piano, I felt the most at ease in this new home since my arrival.

I did not know what time it was, but something woke me and I startled. Rain was blowing in my bedroom window. I quickly rushed to shut it, and then I saw what had awakened me; it was hail - every farmer's nightmare for his crops. "My garden!" I whispered. At once I was running down the stairs and out the back door, grabbing an empty wash tub and rushing barefooted in the rain, hail pelting my head and arms as I frantically tried to cover as many plants with the metal tub as I could. I rushed through the darkness; my only light was the distant lightning. I reached the back porch, grabbed a wooden crate, and headed back to the garden again, placing the crate over as many plants as I could.

Reaching for another empty crate, warm hands grabbed my shoulders. "What do you think you are doing?" Keane asked.

"Saving my garden!" I said, pulling away from him and running back to the garden. I had just placed the crate over several of the tomato plants when he swept me up into his arms. Muddy feet and all, he ran with me as hail pelted my body. He had been smart enough to grab his work hat, and I tucked my head against his neck to seek the protection it offered. He set me down on the porch, and Mormor wrapped a blanket about my shoulders.

In the kitchen I wrapped my hair in a towel and sat at the table defeated, knowing he would not let me back out there. I watched the destruction out the window covered in cheery red, gingham curtains. "Look at you! You could have been killed!" Keane said, lifting my arm to where whelps were swelling up all over. "Do not ever scare me like that again!" he said, aggravated, and left Mormor and me as he headed back upstairs.

Tears filled my eyes, but not at his words; they were tears of worry for what the hail could do to our wheat and crops and my father's as well. "God is in control, Georgiana; He will take care of us. Now go get dry and try to get some sleep," she said, placing a kiss on my cheek. I nodded and slowly made my way to my room, changing into a dry gown and squeezing out the water from my hair, brushing it out to dry. My skin tingled from where I had been pelted so many times by the hail. I would look ridiculous for the dance that evening. For hours to come, I couldn't help but lay awake and pray.

I had just taken the biscuits from the oven when Keane and Henry came in. Keane immediately came and took my hands in his. "The damage is not too bad; God was with us. I rode over to your father's; his damage was even less than ours. I think it is going to be all right," he said tenderly.

I gasped in air, not realizing that in my worry, I tended not to breathe deeply. Tears filled my eyes; I nodded and thanked him. To my surprise, he hugged me closely, for only a few seconds, and then released me. He stood at the back door with a cup of coffee and smiled. "Your garden survived despite your attempts at suicide," he chuckled. I dried my eyes quickly and served breakfast, a much needed peace filling my heart.

The morning was nice and cool as I straightened my garden to its rights and weeded the front flower beds. A few of Mormor's peonies were bent, but the crops would survive and I was thankful. I began to sing praises out loud, rejoicing in our good fortune. Keane walked past me and smiled, shaking his handsome head as if he thought I was crazy, singing to the top of my lungs as I weeded the beds. I still had a few whelps on my arms, but I was hopeful that by this evening they would disappear. I was now even more excited for the dance.

I spent the afternoon baking pies for the dance. Keane and I had gone straight after dinner and picked blackberries, and now I quickly set to baking them into delicious pies. I pulled the tub off the back porch and put on water to boil for a bath. After washing my hair, Mormor insisted on rolling it for me in rags. I let it dry in the heat of the kitchen as I finished my baking then went upstairs to my room.

A knock sounded at my door. Thinking Mormor had come to help me take the rags out of my hair, I called for her to come in as I made up my bed with clean sheets. I looked over to see Keane smiling mischievously. I squealed and grabbed the quilt in front of me. He laughed hysterically. "What on earth is in your hair?" he asked, laughing so hard he held his stomach now.

My cheeks went crimson. "Rag curlers, do you not have any sisters?" I asked, perturbed as I tied my dressing gown over my underthings.

"No, I have six brothers," he said, smiling his handsome smile.

I growled at him. "What did you want anyway?" I asked, finishing making my bed.

"To see if you were up for a swim, but I suspect you'd surely drown with all that…rag stuff in your hair," he said teasing. I threw my pillow and to my surprise, I hit him straight in the head. I burst into laughter. So many times I had tried to hit one of my sisters with a pillow to get her to leave me alone, but had always failed, and for the first time my aim was true, hitting my husband of all people.

Keane's look was of pure surprise. I could not stop laughing. "Keep laughing, rag doll!" he said as he walked away. I couldn't help it, but I did. Just wait until Celia learned I could finally hit something that I aimed for.

Mormor gifted me her long oval mirror, and I stood before it, taking in my appearance. I had her help me into my corset but asked that she not tie it nearly as tightly as Celia had on my wedding day. My hair held the most beautiful bouncy curls, and Mormor gathered them loosely behind me with my matching blue ribbon. I put on my new boots and dabbed a little perfume on my neck, knowing how hot it would be inside the Stein's large barn with so many people dancing; I didn't want to smell badly. Keane, too, wore his wedding finery and smiled as he offered me his arm.

"Are you certain you do not want to come along, Mormor?" I asked. She smiled and shook her head.

"Tobias Long is bringing his mother by; she is my dear friend and doesn't get out much. We will enjoy one of those blackberry pies you made. You two run along and have fun," she said as she urged us out the door.

Keane helped me up into the buggy and went back for the pies covered with cheesecloth. I was anxious to see my family; it had been five days, the longest I had ever been away from them. Keane sat next to me and smiled. "You look happy tonight. Although I still think the rags added a little something," he teased.

I playfully smacked him on the arm. It was sort of sad that he was my husband and instead it felt as if he might be an older brother, if I would have had one. "I am happy. I am anxious to see my sisters and, of course, to dance. I love to dance!" I said, blushing under his gaze. His smiled faded. I reached over and patted his arm tenderly. "I am sorry for you, Keane. I have no right to feel so happy when you are so miserable missing her," I said softly.

He looked at me with such surprise. "I want you to be happy, Georgiana," he said, softly making my stomach flutter. How could he do it so easily?

"And I want you to be happy as well. I tell you what, tonight, every time a thought of the lovely Melody enters your head, I want you to grab the first girl you see and swing her out onto the dance floor, but make certain to only dance the fast dances or group dances. It will help you to forget her," I said, hoping I was right.

He chuckled softly. "And you think that will work?" he asked, raising an eyebrow in question.

I was momentarily stunned by his handsomeness and had to look away. It was a pity he loved another. "Perhaps," I said softly. "I will pray it will," I added.

He surprised me and took me by the hand. "Mormor was right; you have the biggest heart of anyone I have ever known. Most wives would be green with jealously, making their husband's lives miserable if they knew they loved another, but not you, Georgiana, no, never you. Instead you will me to go forward. You are good for me, I think," he said smiling weakly. I squeezed his hand. If only he knew I did have my moments of jealousy. But keeping him at arm's length was also my selfish way of keeping my heart safe from falling in love with him.

"Georgie!" I heard my sister Celia squeal with delight as soon as Keane and I walked into the Stein's large barn.

I hugged her close and marveled at how suddenly grown up she looked. "How are you, sweet Celia?" I asked softly.

Her blush told me everything; she was truly happy. "John, why don't you take Keane over and find Matthias and Drew while we brides catch up?" Celia asked sweetly.

John smiled and kissed her cheek. "As you wish, my lovely bride!" John said, leaving us. I looked to Keane and was surprised he seemed reluctant to leave me. I gave him a little playful wave. He shook his head and smiled.

"Well, you two seem to have worked things out," Eleanor said, as she and Millicent joined us.

I hugged each of them and smiled. It was so good to see them again. "We are getting along which, I suppose, is progress," I admitted.

"Hmmm, just getting along? Sure, Georgie dear," Valynn said, hugging me.

"So Millie, Eleanor, how have you been? I wish you would come for tea; I miss you all so much. And I admit the company would be most welcome," I said.

"Well, we will be meeting in three days at my house for dinner. Do not forget," Eleanor reminded us all.

"I do not know about the other brides, but I am blissfully happy!" Millie said blushing.

"I am, too. Isn't it so wonderful?" Eleanor asked.

"Let's place a small wager just between us girls on who will be with child first!" Celia suggested. My heart fell to my knees, the ugly truth brought back to me so suddenly. I would not be a mother, and I would have to watch as each of my friends carried her babies. Tears filled my eyes as I fought to keep my smile plastered on my face.

"I place my bet on Millie; she comes from a family of eleven. I think it's in her genes," Eleanor laughed.

"Well, I place my bet on Georgie; by the look on Keane's face, I think they are more than getting along," Millie said smiling.

I shook my head no and blushed, but my mind was foggy; if she only knew my husband was more like a brother or cousin to me. I heard the musicians warming up, and suddenly Valynn hooked her arm with mine. "Let's get you some punch, Georgie," she said, getting me away from the conversation.

When we took our glasses of punch, I blushed and thanked her. She looked at me with sorrow in her eyes, but I smiled and looked around the room as if nothing had ever upset me. I married for the farm, and I now had the farm. I should want for nothing else.

I saw from a distance John and Drew claiming their brides for the first dance. The youngest Stein boy, Isaac, came and asked Valynn for the dance. I smiled and took her punch cup and urged her on. Again, I reminded myself why I had married Keane, for my future provision, and the most important reason of all, for my sisters and for their happiness.

"You said to grab the first girl I saw, but I am afraid I only have eyes for one girl tonight," I heard and looked to find Keane standing beside me with that handsome smile of his.

His words were charming, and I smiled and blushed. "So, do you need my help in distracting you?" I asked playfully. He sighed and nodded. I reached over and took his hand in mine. He smiled and led me to the dance floor and twirled me around as we caught the beat of the music. It was a lively dance, and I was thrilled. I myself needed a distraction, and Keane had come just in time.

"Am I helping yet?" I asked, smiling brightly as he whirled me around.

He smiled and pulled me closer. "Too soon to tell, I will need more dances," he teased as the song ended.

We clapped, and I offered him my hands. "Well then, we must dance until you are quite certain," I said smiling.

He pulled me closer and smiled when he realized it was a waltz.

"To help us catch our breaths," he said smiling. I enjoyed dancing with Keane. He was actually quite good; I had to admit I was a little worried over his skill before.

"You know, Georgiana, I find myself amazed. You are quite the lady. You dig in the dirt with your hands, work like a man, play like a child, and sing like an angel. You play the piano better than anyone I have ever heard, and do not even get me started on your cooking," he said laughing. I smiled but my cheeks were warm from such surprising compliments. My heart raced with this change in my husband. But then he sighed deeply. "Why can't I fall madly in love with you?" he asked, looking into my eyes all of a sudden. My enjoyment of the evening, along with my heart, crashed down to the dirt floor. I had to look away. That was the question I had asked myself since Robert had stopped writing to me four years ago. Why couldn't anyone fall in love with me? His arm tightened around my waist and I leaned into him, just needing the support, for my legs felt weak beneath me. He held me closer than needed, deepening the hurt I held inside. I was thankful when the dance ended and we walked to the side to find refreshment. *Perhaps we shouldn't have come at all, I thought to myself.*

"Georgie, with your husband's permission, could I ask for this dance?" I heard as Keane and I both turned to see Robert standing there behind us. I blushed as I looked to Keane. He was not happy about it, but nodded, never taking his eyes from mine. I accepted Robert's hand and allowed him to lead me to the dance floor. "Are you having a good time, *my Georgie?*" he asked tenderly. *My Georgie*, oh how his words made my heart ache. I nodded but must not have been too convincing. "May I ask you a personal question, Georgie?" he asked softly. I nodded but looked around hoping no one had heard. "Is he kind to you? Because sometimes I wonder, by the look on your face, if he treats you well?"

I tried my best to smile. "Keane is kind to me. Ours is a marriage in name only. We were both to inherit Kenrick Farms but had to agree to marry to receive it. He loves another," I forced out softly and immediately regretted it.

He squeezed me tenderly and shook his head. "If only I had come sooner," he whispered. I looked up surprised. "You thought I had forgotten you?" he asked with a tender smile.

I nodded. "You stopped writing to me," I said softly.

He nodded. "I regret that. I suppose I was so busy with medical school. I was studying all hours of the night, trying to finish school two years early. I will be honest, I did not know where my profession would take me, but when the internship here in Crawford opened up, I had to take it. I had to come back and see," he said softly. "Forgive me for being too late?" he asked.

I shook my head, more confused than ever. "There is nothing to forgive," I said softly as the dance ended. We hadn't even made it from the floor when my brother-in-law John asked me to dance, and then Drew and Matthias. I saw Celia pull Keane to the dance floor, but his eyes frantically kept track of where I was. Then Robert came again, and two other gentlemen I did not know. I had to admit my spirits were starting to lift at having so many offers to dance, and there was nothing like music to lift one's spirit. I might not have a loving marriage, but I was not a spinster. At least to common knowledge I wasn't.

Soon Keane found me and to my surprise, he held on to me tightly. He leaned in close and whispered into my ear. "Let us go outside for some fresh air," he suggested, and I nodded, needing to feel a cool breeze. "Are you having fun? You look like you are; I have hardly been able to dance with you," he said softly.

I turned and looked at him. "There are other girls to dance with, my sisters perhaps," I said, not wishing him to be left alone.

He pulled me closer. "But only you can help me forget her," he whispered.

It should have made me feel better, but instead, it hurt me to know he merely meant to replace Melody with me. I pulled back a little. "I do not think I am able to help you much," I confessed and took a deep breath of the night air.

"If you cannot help me, no one can," he said with a heavy sigh.

"God can!" I said, growing irritated at him.

"Yes, you are right, of course," he said.

"You have to want to forget her, Keane," I whispered. He pulled me into his embrace, and oh how good it felt to be held. I could not help but hug him back. It just felt so right, and different, definitely not a brotherly feeling.

"Help me want to forget," he pleaded into my hair.

"I cannot," I whispered. "I am not enough," I added with a broken voice. I quickly pulled away and rushed back inside where Valynn pulled me into a group dance against my protests. Seconds later, I looked up to find Keane had followed me, a look of sorrow on his face.

I hugged my family goodbye, and my mother softly asked if I was holding up all right. I smiled and nodded. "It hasn't been bad," I assured her. She looked worried, but Eleanor and Millie ran up to bid us goodnight and to remind us to be at Eleanor's at six sharp Tuesday night. We drove home in silence. Keane did not speak until we were near our farm. "Dr. Anderson seemed quite serious when he first danced with you; you all talked nearly the entire time," he stated rather bluntly.

I looked over to him. "How can you be so jealous of something you care nothing about?" I asked hurt.

"I am not jealous," he said firmly. I shrugged and looked away.

"I just wondered what he could possibly have to say and noticed just how much he had to say to *my* wife," he added, not letting it go.

"I don't want to fight with you," I said sighing.

"I am not fighting; but why won't you tell me what he said?" he asked, getting riled up.

"Fine! He asked if I was happy because it doesn't appear to him that I am. He asked if you treated me kindly. He told me the only reason he returned to Crawford was to see if I had changed, if I was still the same girl as I was four years ago. He said he was sorry he was too late, for when he arrived, I had just married you," I shouted out angrily.

Keane stopped the buggy and turned towards me. "You see, I told you he was in love with you," he declared.

I frowned. "You never told me that," I insisted.

"Well, I told you he thought you were beautiful, same thing." His profile was amplified by the moonlight. Why did he have to be so handsome?

"It is not the same thing! You said I was lovely, but yet you're in love with another; it is not the same thing!" I yelled in return.

"What did you tell him, when he asked if I was kind?" he demanded.

I sighed trying to calm my temper and closed my eyes. "I told him yes, you were kind," I replied.

He nodded and thanked me. "Is that all he said?" he asked, sighing.

I shrugged. "He asked something about why I seemed unhappy and how you do not seem too fond of me, and I told him why we married, for the farm," I said softly.

"What? You told him about the farm, that we have a marriage in name only?" he asked, angry.

"Yes, I told him. The whole town knows it anyway. And believe me, if they didn't, within a few months they will, after the other brides start announcing they are expecting and I do not for years to come!" I yelled and then broke down crying.

"That's just great!" he said, slapping his hat on his leg. "He will try and take you away now, knowing you are not in love with me," he said softly.

I kept crying. "He is not like that, Keane," I assured him through my tears.

"Georgiana, I am sorry, please do not cry. Come here, I am sorry," he said, pulling me to him and holding me. I held onto him and wept, my heart breaking. Robert seemed interested in me; I must have truly let the desires of having my own farm, the Kenrick farm, blind me from God's will. "Forgive me," he whispered into my hair, and to my surprise, he kissed my forehead.

"I do not understand you, Keane," I confessed between my tears.

He sighed and held me even tighter. "I do not even understand myself anymore, sweetheart," he whispered.

CHAPTER FIVE

The next morning was church. I dressed in my lavender gown with lace overlay, and yes, the corset as well. I was up early, not having slept well, and set about making cinnamon toast and oatmeal for a quick and easy breakfast. Conversations with Keane the night before plagued me, especially the part when he begged me to help him want to forget Melody. What did that even mean? He either wanted to forget her or he didn't. By now she was married to his brother.

Mormor came out dressed for church and hugged me tightly. "How did the dance go?" she asked, taking her toast and tea to the table. I nodded, but not excitedly. She frowned. "It did not bring you two any closer?" she asked, disappointed.

I gave her a weak smile and shook my head no. She sighed heavily. "I am trying, Mormor. I just do not know what he needs or wants. He confuses me," I confessed but quickly hushed as Keane and Henry came in from doing chores. Keane blushed and smiled weakly at me and thanked me for breakfast. Then to my surprise, he kissed my cheek. I stood frozen as my eyes met his, and he gave me a wink. Oh, how he infuriated me!

We met John and Celia and walked into church with them and sat down next to them as we greeted Eleanor and Matthias. Mormor sat with my parents and Henry. Keane took my hand in his, and I looked up in surprise. He placed a soft kiss on my knuckles, and I had to look away lest he see the blush covering my face and neck. What had happened to him overnight, or was this just a show for everyone else? I quickly looked around but did not see Robert anywhere. Then I looked back to Keane and his look was soft and tender.

We shared a hymnal as we rose to sing; his hand went to the small of my back, doing strange things to my insides. After church my parents invited us home for dinner, along with Henry and Mormor, but I had placed a ham in the oven before we left, so I kissed my mother's cheeks and promised to come next Sunday.

Back at the farmhouse I hurried to serve dinner and sat down as we all held hands to pray. "I am thankful for Georgie's cooking," Henry said with a smile.

Keane frowned. "How come he gets to call you Georgie?" he asked.

I blushed. "Henry has known me since I was a child. He is like my uncle, and he loves me," I said lamely. I could tell this didn't sit well with my husband. Mormor looked amused.

After dinner I cleaned the dishes and was headed upstairs to rest. "How about a swim?" I heard Keane ask from the bottom of the stairs.

I sighed. "I feel rather tired today," I offered softly.

"It is too hot to rest upstairs. Bring along a quilt, and after we swim, we can nap in the shade," he said with a hopeful glint in his eyes. I knew the swimming diversion helped get Keane's mind off his troubles, and it *was* hot.

"All right, let me change." I heard him go into his room to change as well, and I grabbed an older quilt from my trunk and met him in the kitchen. We rode out to the swimming hole, and after I had changed and was safely in the water, Keane joined me. Why was it only here that he was so charming and relaxed? We took turns swinging from the rope until my arms ached and I insisted I had to rest.

I spread out my quilt under the large shade tree and collapsed wearily. The summer breeze felt wonderful across my wet skin. I found myself drifting off to sleep quickly.

"Georgiana," I heard Keane whisper.

I turned to find him sitting beside me. "Yes?" I asked.

"I am sorry for last night; I didn't mean to ruin your evening," he said softly.

I shrugged and closed my eyes. "You didn't ruin my evening; I had fun, at times. You just confuse me. But our situation is difficult, and any stress it causes, I deserve," I said yawning.

"You do not deserve my moodiness, and you were right. I was jealous," he confessed.

My eyes opened in shock at his revelation. "You said you never lie," I said softly.

"I know, and I normally don't. Why do I find myself lying to you?" he asked, sounding as confused as I felt.

"Why were you jealous?" I asked turning towards him. "You're in love with Melody. Why care who appreciates me or dances with me? I do not understand," I said, needing to try and figure this man out before he drove me insane.

Keane sighed. "I think it is because I am beginning to see she would never have made it here. She is a city girl; she would never help milk a cow, tend a garden, or take care of Mormor. At times I almost resent you for her short comings. It is wrong of me. I am sorry," he said so tenderly.

I could not help but reach over to him and take his hand in mine. "Perhaps this is part of your healing process," I said, squeezing his hand warmly.

He nodded and gave me a mischievous smile. "I realized I was jealous for certain last night when he held you in his arms," he said looking away.

"Robert?" I asked, feeling all warm inside.

He nodded. "You cared for him; he gets to call you Georgie," he said with a chuckle. He squeezed my hand, and I knew he was serious.

"Perhaps I allow him to call me Georgie because we are old friends or because I know he cannot break my heart," I said, sighing and feeling so tired and weary of this confusion but still trying to please Keane.

"And I cannot call you Georgie because....?" he asked tenderly.

I quickly turned over on my side and closed my eyes. "Because... you could...break my heart," I whispered, drifting off to sleep.

Suddenly I awoke to cold water dribbling on my face and legs; I gasped as I struggled to wake. "Keane!" I screamed as I realized he was dripping water from his hat to wake me up.

"Time to wake up, sleeping Georgiana! We had best head home. You have slept the afternoon away, and I am afraid you might be dehydrating," he said laughing.

"Well, you didn't have to wake me up by dripping cold water on me! You are so mean!" I said standing to my feet angry, my heavy hair swinging behind me.

"You're awful cute when you're mad," he laughed.

I stomped my foot and growled. He raised an eyebrow at me and grinned his handsome grin. "Be careful or I am liable to slap that handsome grin off your face!" I threatened before I could catch myself.

He smiled. "So you think I am handsome, do you?" he asked teasing.

"No, I do not!" I said, folding the quilt and gathering up my dress to put back on.

"Here let me help you….," Keane said. Suddenly he scooped me into his arms and ran down to the creek and threw me in backside first as I screamed. "Let me help you cool off," he said laughing.

I came out of the water spluttering. "Oh you have had it now, Keane Kenrick! I would be afraid if I were you," I said, climbing out of the creek where he rolled on the grass laughing. "No pie for you!" I said, gathering my dress up and squeezing out the water from my hair.

"Oh no! Anything but the pie! You know how I love your pies, Georgiana; take anything from me but pie," he teased.

I couldn't help but smile. "You're incorrigible *and* infuriating!" I complained.

"And you are breathtaking all wet and mad," he said so tenderly, that for a moment, I thought he might kiss me. But instead he offered me his hand and helped me onto my horse. "I wouldn't break your heart, you know, not on purpose anyway," he said, taking my hand and startling me.

I could only nod, not able to catch my breath. And then, before he could mount his horse, I called out, "Race you home!" I took off at full gallop, my heart racing. I had to get away from him.

"You're an excellent seamstress, Mormor," I said, smiling as she held up one of my new dresses made in the sage green material trimmed with lace.

"I will make you a deal; I will do all the sewing if you keep making these pies. I do have such a sweet tooth," she confessed. I smiled, knowing Keane and Henry had been enjoying them as well. "I thought you might want to wear this one tonight to Eleanor's," she said, holding it up to me.

"I would love to, thank you so much!" I said, hugging her tightly. "I have baked us a strawberry pie and a blackberry pie, and I am taking this peach cobbler to Eleanor's," I said, with a wipe to my sweaty forehead. I had done laundry nearly half the day before and then after another swim came home to pick more produce from the garden and help Keane start on the sleeping porch. Today, as I looked out the kitchen window, it looked as if we might get rain. I prayed for a good gentle soaking. The earth was dry and the air was much too hot. In just a few hours we were due at Eleanor's, and I was excited to see Celia again. I missed her dearly and, of course, Eleanor and Millie as well, but I needed some time with my sister, to talk with her over all these things going on with Keane. He was still so confusing. One minute I felt he might like me, another minute perhaps just tolerate me, and then at times I felt he resented the sight of me. He was so infuriating!

Suddenly I saw him sit on the back porch to take his dirty work boots off, and I smiled. Turning, I grabbed the metal pail with fresh, cool well water and winked at Mormor as I opened the screen door softly and dumped the pail over his head, just as he turned around. He gasped, and I burst into laughter as his shocked face met mine. "I told you that you should be afraid," I said, nearly doubled over laughing. I could see Henry laughing by the fence and heard Mormor's gentle laughter behind me.

Before I could back my way into the kitchen, Keane swung me over his shoulder and stood rushing towards the barn. I was squealing for him to put me down in between my laughter and his wet shirt soaking through my apron. Where was he taking me? What was in the barn except for manure? Oh no!

"Keane, we are due at Eleanor's in just a few hours! Please put me down! We are even now," I pleaded, still laughing. He shut the barn door behind him and pulled me to his chest. I could not help but keep laughing. Instantly his lips claimed mine, and I could scarcely breathe. His arms held me tightly to his chest, and I could feel his heart racing and knew mine was as well. My arms instinctively went around his neck, and he intensified the kiss, making my knees weak.

He pulled back just a little and smiled. "Now you have done it, Mrs. Kenrick," he whispered. I couldn't say anything. I had no idea kissing could be like that. Before I could defend myself, he lifted me up in his arms, my heart raced at his nearness. I longed to kiss him again, but then, splash! Laughing, he dunked me in the horse trough. I came up spluttering and screaming.

"Oops, I am coming, Mormor," he said, racing towards the house as Henry opened the door.

"Keane! Help me out of here!" I screamed, so angry with him. How dare he kiss me like that and then dump me in the nasty horse water.

Henry was laughing as he came and helped me out of the trough. "Just wait until he is milking, Georgie. I'll leave that pile of dung in the corner there. You sneak upon him and shove him in," he said, laughing so hard he nearly knocked us both over.

I smiled. "Thank you Henry, I do believe I will," I said determined.

I quickly washed my hair and body with the scented soap, cringing to think my entire body had been drown in horse drool. Mormor had not seen Keane when I reached the house drenched, and she had been kind enough to hand me a clean dress and under things on the back porch, along with soap and a few towels. I had come to bathe and swim alone, and by my apparent anger, I knew Mormor would not ask Keane to follow me. How could he kiss me like that and then dump me in the trough? Had he not enjoyed the kiss? Was I a terrible kisser? That was my first true kiss except for the two small ones he had given me at our weddings. Surely I could improve with time if he gave me a chance. But he wouldn't, and I wouldn't let him; those kisses were exactly what would break my heart.

The sun was completely gone now behind dark clouds, and I smiled as I felt the gentle rain beat down on my face as I swam: I needed to return now or we would be late to Eleanor's, and we couldn't be late. I desperately needed to talk to the other brides. Had they experienced any problems or quarrels with their husbands the past two weeks? I was certain they hadn't been dumped into a horse trough.

"Swimming in the rain?" I heard and I closed my eyes. Of all the nerve, he had followed me. "Mind if I clean off before we ride over to the Stein's?" he asked carefully.

"I would rather you not, at least until I am out. If you turn around, I will step out and you can have the entire place to yourself," I said coldly.

"I do not want the entire place to myself," he said with a smirk.

"Well, I am sorry, but I must insist you do today," I said raising my chin higher. "Please turn around."

"Awe, Georgiana, you're not still mad at me because I kissed you and gave you a swim in the horse trough, are you?" he asked with that dad-blasted smile.

"Of course not! Every bride wants to be kissed just like that, and then dumped in horse drool, or worse," I said spitefully. He chuckled and began walking toward me, taking off his shirt. "Keane, please turn around. I cannot swim with you today," I said pleading.

He frowned. "I will stay on my side of the hole, just keep me company. I promise I won't kiss you again if it upset you so much," he said disappointed.

"This is not about the kiss, we can discuss that later. Please give me some privacy," I pleaded. He took down his britches and I turned around, knowing he was still in his underthings. I was angry he wasn't listening to me. I heard the water stir. "Keane! I do not have my underthings on because they were slimy with horse drool!" I yelled with my back still toward him, water up to my neck.

I heard the water swooshing as he climbed back onto the bank. "I am sorry, Georgiana; it is safe. I have the quilt held out and my back turned," he said frustrated.

I turned to look and, of course, he had told the truth. I rushed out onto the bank, yanking the quilt from him and wrapping up quickly. I grabbed my fresh clothing and rushed behind the tree. "All right, you can get in the water now," I called to him once I was dressed. I heard a splash and knew he was in the water, so I came out from behind the tree and walked toward my horse, my hair wrapped in a towel.

"Will you wait for me?" he asked as he took up the soap. I turned my head.

"Why must I wait for you?" I asked like a pouting child.

"No reason. I just enjoy our time together here. But go on home; I will be there shortly," he said defeated.

I sighed. "If you hurry, I will stay," I agreed and sat down on the bank sticking my feet back into the water. He smiled, and I wondered what on earth we would do when it was too cold this winter to come and swim. So far it was the only way we could enjoy one another's friendship.

Watching his bare muscular back was torture, so I lay back on the soft grass enjoying the cool water on my feet, and looked up to the cloudy sky. It had merely sprinkled before, but I hoped these clouds brought more of the much needed moisture we prayed for.

"Georgiana, are you angry that I kissed you?" I heard him ask as he came out of the water and dried off. I closed my eyes and heard him laugh. "What a sight you are lying in the grass, your bare feet in the water and that big towel in your hair," he chuckled tenderly.

I slapped at the air hoping to hit him, but knew he was too far from me, but I wasn't about to open my eyes. "No, I am not upset that you kissed me. Surprised perhaps, but not upset," I said softly with a sigh.

"I was surprised, too," he said dressing.

"Why did you kiss me, Keane, and then dump me in the trough? You promised you wouldn't break my heart," I said softly.

"I didn't mean to hurt you. I am sorry if I did," he said tenderly. I sighed. That was even worse; he regretted the kiss.

"I am dressed," he said softly, and I sat up. Suddenly his hand was helping me up as I grabbed the towel to steady it on my head. Our eyes met, but I quickly looked away. It hurt too much to know he was disappointed in me. Had he compared my kiss to Melody's? "I had to do something," he said softly, nervously, as he still held my hand. I looked at him confused. "Or else, I might have kept kissing you," he whispered.

My mouth opened in shock. "So, it wasn't because, because I couldn't kiss like Melody? That was my first true kiss," I stammered, truly nervous now.

Keane's face softened even more, and he pulled me into his embrace and held me. "No, I did not compare you to her. That is what frightened me; she never even entered my mind," he said, holding me. I hugged him back, tears filling my eyes. Something was changing between us, and it frightened me, too. He helped me onto my horse and smiled. "I am glad I was your first true kiss," he said, smiling his handsome smile as if it were some kind of honor to be my first kiss. I blushed, and once again I took off to the house at a full gallop, leaving him to follow in my dust.

Matthias and Eleanor's house sat on a parcel of land that Matthias and John's parents owned. I smiled as I took in the pale blue paint and white shutters of the small cottage. I had yet to even see Celia's home and wondered why she had not invited Keane and me to dinner. Of course, I had not invited her and John to Kenrick Farms either. Keane looked handsome in a white shirt and starched denims that I had not seen him wear yet. I wore my new summer dress with the short puffed sleeves and bustle that Mormor had made from the sage green material that my sister Augusta had chosen for me. I wore my hair up tonight, as most married women did, *and* because I did not have time to properly dry and curl it after my bath since I had waited and kept Keane company at the swimming hole. But I had to smile; at least he wasn't disgusted by my kiss and wished to spend time with me.

"You look lovely tonight, Mrs. Kenrick," Keane whispered into my ear as he helped me down from the buggy, with the sound of thunder rumbling in the back ground.

I blushed as Eleanor greeted us at the door, and John went with Keane to situate our horses. "What a lovely dress, Georgie!" Eleanor said, hugging my neck.

"Thank you, Eleanor." I had barely spoken when I heard my sister call.

"Georgie!" Celia squealed with delight. I hugged her warmly and smiled as I took in the cozy cottage with blue gingham curtains and oak furniture.

"Celia, where is your home located?" I asked as I followed the ladies into the parlor.

"Come," she said, leading me to the side window. "About a mile west, sometimes you can see our lights from here," she said, glowing with happiness.

Millie came in and greeted us. "Look at this peach cobbler Georgie made," she said, setting it on the counter in the kitchen.

"My favorite!" Celia said, bouncing up and down.

"I will not get to see you on your birthday; you will spend it at the Falls," I said, enjoying her excitement.

"As soon as we return from our wedding trip, and Matthias and Eleanor return from theirs, we must meet again, but this time at John's and my home. I hope to have exciting news to tell by then!" Celia whispered the last part.

"Not already!" Millie gasped and then giggled.

"John and Celia have barely stepped a foot from their home the past two weeks," Eleanor teased.

"Of course, it is too soon to tell," I said softly. Celia shrugged with a giddy smile.

The front door opened as the men stepped inside, cutting off our private conversations. We sat down in the dining room, and Matthias led the blessing over our food. Pleasant conversation drifted throughout the cottage for several hours as a hard rain fell outside.

"Keane, you know you married the best cook in Lowe County, no offense, Sweetheart," Drew said with a grin as Millie slapped his arm.

I blushed, and to my surprise Keane's arm went around my shoulders warmly. "I do know, and I am lucky. A different kind of pie every night keeps a man satisfied," he said with a chuckle.

"Well, I say the next dinner should be at Kenrick Farms, say tomorrow night," Matthias teased. I laughed.

"You are all most welcome at any time," I offered. Keane smiled at me with what looked like husbandly pride. It made me warm and tingly inside. After the rain slowed and the dishes cleared, the men excused themselves to check the livestock.

I quickly pulled Celia aside in the hallway near the washroom. "Please come visit me soon. I am so confused and need someone to talk to," I said pleading to my sister who apparently, despite being younger, knew more about men than I.

"We heard that, Georgie! Come in here, in my room," Eleanor giggled from the kitchen. She quickly ushered us all into the bedroom.

"But what if they come back?" I asked nervously.

"They will merely think we are talking girl stuff, or that I am showing you around the house. You know they are out there doing the same thing," Eleanor said, making me sit on the edge of the bed. "All right, Georgie, now what is going on? Keane put his arm around you, and he looks at you like a man in love," Eleanor demanded.

Celia bounced happily, and I sighed and shook my head. "No, it isn't love. It is very confusing. You know he is in love with Melody," I said.

"He thinks he is," Millie said with a giggle.

"Well, he has been acting strangely, and the night of the dance, he became so jealous over Robert Anderson. It was ridiculous. And then we argued, and I told him he had to want to get over Melody. And he pleaded with me to help him to want to get over her. I was so confused. What does that mean? Then, today in the barn, he kissed me. It was not a little peck, mind you. I thought my knees would buckle. And then…he threw me into the horse trough to pay me back for dumping cold water on him earlier," I said breathlessly.

Celia jumped to her feet. "He kissed you and then dumped you in a horse trough?" she asked, furious.

I nodded but told her to sit down. I wasn't finished. "Then, he followed me out to the creek where I was bathing, and I asked him why he kissed me and dumped me in the trough. He said he had to before he did something else. I had been terribly upset all afternoon, thinking that I had been horrible at kissing or that he was comparing me to Melody. But he honestly told me that it was because if he didn't, he would not have been able to stop kissing me. And that he hadn't thought of Melody at all. Help me! What do I do?" I asked, panicked.

They were all smiling now. "First, you do as he asked; you help him want to forget her. Be bold and kiss him. Make his favorite foods. Do little things to help him. Compliment him," Eleanor said.

"And I think we need Dr. Anderson to make a call soon. Is your throat hurting, Georgie?" Millie asked me.

I gasped. "No! Not that! Not Robert! Keane was very jealous," I said, not wanting to replay that night.

"It is good for him to see what he could be missing," Celia smiled.

"You mentioned the other day how he likes to go swimming; suggest that he take you on a midnight swim," Millie said giggling. I gasped again.

"Well, Valynn isn't here, so I have to speak for her," she said, smiling and blushing.

"Hold his hand on the way home tonight in the buggy, and sit real close," Eleanor giggled. We heard a door shut, and we all sat still.

"Ellie, are you ladies all right in there?" Matthias asked.

"Yes! We are coming," she said, and we all burst into giggles.

"Hang in there, Georgie, he is coming around!" Millie whispered.

Celia hugged me. "Just think Georgie, we could be mothers together by this time next year," she said excitedly.

"We only just kissed today," I giggled. I loved these women more than life itself.

Once the rain slowed down, we left for home. Keane was especially quiet on the drive, and I wondered if he had enjoyed his time with the men. "John and Matthias seem very nice, and Drew as well," I said, breaking the silence.

Keane looked to me and nodded. "Yes, they are all good men. Friendly," he said but said no more for several minutes. "They sure like your cobbler," he said, gently elbowing me. I smiled and blushed. "I did, too," he added.

"Thank you," I said, elbowing him back. "It was a lovely evening," I said with a sigh of contentment. It had been lovely seeing my sister and friends again. I had missed spending time with them. He only nodded. I couldn't help but wonder what the men talked of outside for so long. Maybe Keane was thinking of Melody. I couldn't help but feel let down at the thought.

Lightening flashed in the distance. "Best hurry these horses on home. Looks as if we are in for another storm," he said, tensing up.

"Perhaps it is just heat lightening," I said hopeful. He nodded, but I saw his concern. We were edging into the middle of August and the harvest was near. We could only pray for good weather. With the worry of bad weather, I completely forgot Eleanor's advice about holding my husband's hand.

Keane started to pull me up to the front door of our farmhouse, but I insisted he let me try to cover some of the garden before the storm came. He was busy putting the horses away when the lightning struck close. I heard his voice boom from the barn yard. "Georgiana, best get in the house, you've done all you can," he said, rushing toward me. He quickly took my arm, and we went inside to find Henry and Mormor with a cup of coffee at the kitchen table.

"Looks like you beat the storm," Mormor said, kissing both our cheeks. "How did it go?" she asked.

"It was lovely," I said smiling.

"Would you like coffee?" Keane asked me.

"No thank you, I shall have a hard time sleeping as it is," I said shivering. I was a little frightened as I heard the wind pick up outside.

"Well, I had best get out to the barn before it hits," Henry said, wishing us all a good night. Henry had a large room off the side of the barn in which he had lived for many years.

"You are welcome to stay in a guest room, Henry," Keane said thoughtfully.

"Naw, I am fine, like being where I can listen for the animals. Good night, All," he bid us. Mormor wished us both a good night, but Keane and I just sat at the table, watching the coming storm outside the window.

"Isn't it funny, how something so beautiful can be so frightening?" I whispered as the lightening flashed a brilliant pink just over in the wheat fields.

"I was just thinking the same thing," Keane said, and I found he was watching me. Did he mean I was beautiful or frightening? "You have given up so much to have your share in this farm," he whispered, reaching for my hand.

My eyes met his nervously. What did he mean? "And you lost a great deal when you chose to claim your share," I whispered. "You lost your love, your heart, and your dreams."

He released my hand and leaned back and sighed. "And you lost the hope of having a man to love you, a man to hold you at night, to give you children. I didn't realize until tonight, Georgiana, being around the other couples, just how much you sacrificed. I can only wonder if it was worth it," he asked softly.

My cheeks burned crimson, and my heart ached as I stood to leave. "Goodnight, Keane," I said, rushing away as the tears fell. I had been wrong. We were not drawing closer, and he had just proclaimed everything I had lost, not once offering to fill any of the vacancies. I quickly changed into my nightgown and crawled into bed. As the wind began to roar outside, I was thankful the noise would drown out the sobs that revealed my heart had been torn in two.

It was just after midnight, and the storm still raged. Although I couldn't see any lightening, the wind and thunder were still going strong. I don't know why I woke up so afraid after being asleep only a few hours, perhaps because I had never weathered such a storm alone. I had always known Celia was nearby. But the more the wind roared against my window, the more panicked I became, like I was wearing that blasted corset again. My room was quite warm, so I put my lightweight dressing robe on, tied it and took my pillow downstairs to the parlor which sat on the opposite side of the house. I could still hear the wind, but it wasn't as frightening in the parlor, so I lay on the sofa to sleep. Keane's words from just hours ago still haunted me. What had I gotten myself into? Was this farm worth it? Was fulfilling two older people's wishes worth it?

Would my sisters even appreciate this sacrifice I had made for them? Tears streamed down my cheeks. Had I been meant for Robert? But there was only one face I saw when I closed my eyes.

"Georgiana," his whisper startled me. He was kneeling beside me in the dark. "Are you all right? Did the storm frighten you?" he asked tenderly.

I shook my head. His thumb wiped away a tear, and I knew that he knew I was lying. "Please go away," I whispered. I was ashamed of the mess we were in and ashamed that I wasn't enough for him. But mostly, I was ashamed that I let myself care.

"Shhh," he said, kissing my forehead. "Here, allow me," he said, gently raising me up. I had no idea what he was talking about until he lifted me onto his lap and held me close like a baby. "Just sleep," he whispered into my hair.

Impossible I thought. I had never been so close to a man except earlier in the day, in the barn, when Keane had kissed me and held me close. "But you must get your sleep," I said, nervously trying to sit up.

He held me firm and then lay me in front of him as he lay behind me, with his arm around me on the large sofa. He laid his head against mine. "I can sleep now," he whispered. Oh how I wish Eleanor and Celia could talk to me; I hadn't had a chance to put any of their advice into action yet. I had never felt so warm and safe and couldn't resist snuggling closer to him and closing my eyes as he held me tenderly. Within minutes I could tell he slept, and I closed my eyes, savoring every minute I had in his arms, for when morning came, I had no idea which side of Keane's personality would greet me.

The next morning over breakfast Keane and Henry discussed the new horse stables Keane wished to build. "I would like to telegraph my father and have him send Gaspard out on the next train," Keane said, thanking me as I refilled his coffee cup.

"You mean you would start the stables before harvest?" I asked, surprised. Keane nodded.

"But that is only a little over two weeks away. Does that give you enough time to finish it?" I asked concerned.

By the look on his face, he didn't want my opinion. "You think I am rushing it?" he asked uneasily.

I shrugged. "I just thought perhaps it might be a project you started once harvest was in. Or perhaps after you have had time to pray more about it," I said, starting to wash the dishes.

Henry and Mormor excused themselves quickly. Both said that they had things waiting on them, but Keane remained at the table, glaring at me. "You do not want me to build the stables?" he asked.

I turned in shock. "Of course, I do. I just feel like it is best we wait until harvest and pray about it. It will cost a great deal of money, and I would feel better knowing that money was secure in the bank after this last crop of wheat," I said softly. Keane nodded. "I want you to have your horses, Keane; I do want you to be happy," I said tenderly.

He gave me a weak smile. "Come and pray with me," he said, holding out his hand to me. I was greatly touched and took his hand and knelt beside him at the kitchen table as he prayed and asked God for wisdom, for His favor, and for His timing.

When he finished praying, I surprised myself by kissing his cheek. "Thank you," I said, returning to my chores. Keane still looked troubled as he left for the barn, and I worried that he felt I was trying to ruin his plans, his dreams. First he lost Melody, and now I feared that he felt he had lost his stable and horses as well. I prayed throughout my morning. I prayed for Keane and his happiness and for God to grant us both wisdom and patience.

He didn't speak to me again that day, not one word. He did not come and ask me to join him to swim. The house seemed so quiet, and if it were not for Mormor, I would have felt completely alone.

CHAPTER SIX

The next few days I threw myself into working. I was desperate for an escape from the ups and downs and confusion that came with my husband. I cleaned the upstairs from ceiling to floor, rearranged the layout of the bedrooms, made curtains out of scrap material for Keane's room, and added one of my own homemade quilts to his bed. Downstairs, Mormor and I rearranged the parlor, took down the curtains, washed them, and hung them to dry. I baked from early morning hours until noon, and then again, once the day cooled down.

"You are doing too much, Georgie; you will wear yourself out before harvest comes," Mormor said, pleading for me to rest. But I couldn't rest, not even at night, not unless I worked myself into extreme exhaustion. The cellar shelves were now full, and I was thankful as my garden work was starting to slow down a little. I knew I had preserved enough to safely see us through winter and until the next spring.

I decided the kitchen needed a fresh coat of paint, and I worked at putting fresh white paint onto the walls, then washed and ironed the red gingham curtains I adored so much. Keane had not asked me to swim again, nor had he asked my help with the sleep porch but had sought out Henry's help instead.

When Mormor had the last of my new dresses made, she scowled at me and shook her finger. "Look how much weight you have lost!" She pulled out the sides of my new dress she had measured me for just two weeks ago. I couldn't seem to slow down. I didn't want to slow down. It was as if I was trying to prove something, and yet I didn't know what it was. A visit from my mother and sisters cheered me, but as soon as they left, I once again threw myself into work, tackling the flower beds, weeding and hauling numerous buckets of water. The flower beds were thriving, but I wasn't.

Then came the morning when I could not physically get out of bed. My entire body hurt. I felt something was wrong and forced myself to the washroom, only to find my womanly time had come, but something was not right. It was much more severe than normal. My legs trembled as I made it back to my room. I needed to make breakfast, but I could hardly stand. I closed my eyes, the pain so severe that I thought I might die. Mormor was right; I had been pushing myself too hard. I closed my eyes and awoke later when Mormor knocked on my door, concerned. "Georgie, honey, are you all right?" she asked, coming into my room after I did not answer.

"I am sorry, Mormor; I must have overslept. I awoke earlier, but I am afraid I am not feeling well," I confessed softly.

"No matter, honey; I made breakfast; I can still do that when needed, even if Henry and Keane complain it isn't as tasty as yours. What is wrong, sweetheart? Do you have a fever?" I shook my head no as she felt my forehead. "I have been worried for you; you have been over doing it. I will go and get you some Willow Bark tea and a bite to eat. That should make you feel better," she said, kissing my cheek. I thanked her and quickly fell back asleep.

But to my horror it was not Mormor who brought me the tea and breakfast, it was Keane. "Mormor said you are not well. Should I send for the doctor?" he asked concerned.

I shook my head no. "I will be fine."

"You are terribly pale," he said, looking over me. I frowned. He helped me sit up and laid the tray on my lap. "Shall I feed you?" he asked tenderly.

I blushed. "No! Thank you. I can manage," I said with a weak smile, anything to get him out of my room. He stayed, messing with my covers, fluffing pillows, and feeling my forehead. "Keane, I just need to rest," I said a little irritable with him. He had avoided me since the night he had held me during the storm on the sofa. We had hardly spoken, and I had missed him. Yet I was angry with him as well. With a disappointed look, he nodded and took the tray away. I turned over on my side, feeling a little guilty but too exhausted to think on his moods anymore and soon fell back to sleep.

Soft, cool hands moved across my forehead, and I knew at once my mother was there. I opened my eyes to find her concerned face closely examining mine, with Mormor and Keane leaning over her shoulder. "She doesn't seem to have a fever," Mother said sighing.

"Mother, could I speak with you alone?" I asked near tears.

She nodded, and Mormor had to pull Keane away from my bedside. "Do you think you were with child, Georgie?" she asked gently.

I gasped. "No, no, we haven't….I have been overdoing it, that is all. Mormor warned me to slow down, but I couldn't seem to make myself stop working," I said as the tears fell down my cheeks.

"Oh sweetheart! I wish things were different for you. But I can see a change in Keane. You must be patient, Georgie. He is the one who came for me; he has been beside himself with worry. I think he loves you and is afraid to admit it," she said tenderly. I shook my head no.

"Keane is kind to me, Mother, but he has made it clear that he doesn't want a marriage with me. I have really made a mess of it," I said sobbing. She hugged me closely, kissed my cheek, and cried with me.

A few hours later I tried to stand but gasped with pain in my side and quickly lay back down on the bed. My mother calmly stood and went into the hallway. "I will bring you another cup of tea," she said leaving me. Downstairs I heard her ask Keane to send for Dr. Childers.

I gasped in shock and became angry. "Mother, have you no mercy?" I sobbed when she brought back my tea. "How could you? How embarrassing!" I cried bitterly. I heard a horse ride away and knew soon my humiliation would be complete when Dr. Robert Anderson arrived with Dr. Childers.

Soon I heard Valynn, Genevieve, and Augusta. Mother smiled. "They have come to help with the cooking," she said, trying to soothe me.

"We already have so much food; Georgie has been baking like a raged demon, I tell you," Mormor said concerned. Mother looked at me, her eyes piercing into my soul trying to see what I could possibly be hiding. I closed my eyes and must have fallen asleep, for the next thing I heard was arguing.

"It is best if you remain down here. We will let you see her when our examination is complete." I groaned; it was Robert Anderson.

"My wife is lying up there near to death; my place is with her. If you can be in there, then so can I." And that was Keane. Why was it that when these two men saw one another, it always turned into an argument?

"She isn't going to die, Keane!" That was Valynn, always sensible and matter of fact. Robert came in with Dr. Childers and frowned. Mormor left the room, but I asked my mother to stay.

"Could you have been with child?" Dr. Childers asked. I blushed and shook my head no.

"Our marriage is in name only," I said softly. "I simply over did things, moved heavy furniture when I should have asked for help, washed all the curtains, hauled buckets of water…," Dr. Childers interrupted me with a gentle smile.

"You will not be the first overly ambitious new bride to find herself bedridden," he said tenderly. After visiting with me and pressing on my stomach, he asked Robert for his prognosis.

"Exhaustion and anemia, and it will only get worse for a day or two. My advice would be complete bed rest for a week, light housework with no heavy lifting for two weeks, and an iron remedy," he said with a wink to me.

"I completely concur," Dr. Childers said, standing. "I am turning your care over to Dr. Anderson, Georgie. Do what he says and you will fully recover," he said, patting my hand tenderly. My mother and I thanked him.

"Could I speak with the patient alone?" Robert asked. I blushed and looked at Mother; my eyes begging her to stay.

"Leave the door open," Dr. Childers said with a nod. Mother informed us she would be waiting in the hall; Robert cringed as if that did not give him the privacy he sought.

He sat in the rocking chair next to the bed. "Georgie, you know your happiness affects your health greatly. It is a proven fact." I nodded but remained silent. "You cared for me a little, once, I believe, and perhaps, you might learn to care for me again?" I blushed and went to stop him, but he held his hand up for me to let him finish. "He is overworking you, like a slave. He cares nothing for you. I cannot stand by and allow this to happen," he said firmly.

I shook my head no. "No, you have it all wrong. Keane is kind to me; he is not the one forcing me to work so hard. It is my own doing, I promise. He may love another, but he sees that I am taken care of," I insisted.

Robert shook his head. "No, he doesn't, or you wouldn't be in this condition, Georgie. You deserve to be loved, adored. I can do that, Georgie. I cannot give you a farm, but we could live comfortably in town. I spoke with Celia, and I know the circumstances of this marriage. You are always taking care of others first. Take care of you, Georgie. You can easily have your marriage annulled. I will marry you and transfer my internship to another town so you do not have to face the gossip. We could be happy together," he said tenderly.

It sounded like a fine plan, except for leaving my family, this beloved house, and Keane; for now looking at Robert in this moment, I knew I could not love him. "I cannot leave Keane," I whispered. "Harvest is only a week and a half away."

"Then think upon this, pray about it, and give me your answer after harvest. But Georgie, I warn you, you cannot jump back into working yourself like that. You could ruin your chances of having children one day. I know Keane does not plan to give you children, but if you accept my offer, I will give you as many as you like," he said affectionately. Tears streamed down my face. Why was this happening now? "I will leave you alone, but I want you to consider my offer," he said leaving.

My mother came in as soon as Robert left, and I knew she had heard every tender word he had spoken. "What will you do, my love?" she asked me softly, as if I had an option.

I shook my head and turned away from her. "Are the vows I spoke not worth something; do they not forever bind me to my husband, to a loveless marriage?" I asked, crying.

Suddenly, Keane cleared his voice from the doorway, and I winced, as I knew he had heard my words. "May I see my wife now?" he asked tenderly.

"Of course, Keane. I will go and make you another cup of tea," Mother said, kissing my forehead.

I kept my back to Keane, but he was determined to see me. Sighing, he pulled the rocking chair to the opposite side of the bed. He reached out so tenderly and wiped my tears. I had to close my eyes. "You scared about twenty years off my life," he whispered. Good, I thought silently. Maybe a forty-two year old Keane would be more wise and mature. He leaned in and kissed my forehead. I had the strongest urge to wrap my arms around his neck and not let go. If Eleanor and Mille were there, they would tell me to go ahead, to be bold and hug him closely. But I could not let go of the fact that he had ignored me for days, not even knowing I worked myself into exhaustion. "Can I get you anything?" he asked softly. I shook my head no and kept my eyes closed, hoping he would leave me alone.

"Georgie, you need to wake up and eat, my love," I heard my mother say tenderly. Mother and Mormor were in the room. After helping me to the washroom, I ate the lunch my sisters had made me. "Dr. Anderson said to eat all the meat you can, and he brought back the iron remedy," Mother said, urging me to finish my stew.

"Keane went into town to the butcher, to get us a nice side of beef," Mormor said smiling.

"That was thoughtful of him. I hate to be so much trouble to everyone. I have never been laid up in bed," I said, hating that everyone was so worried over me.

"You need to rest, and we will make certain not to let you have your way again," Mormor said, shaking her finger at me.

I smiled. "I am sorry; you tried so hard to get me to slow down. I promise to listen from now on," I said as she hugged me.

"I love you as my own daughter, Georgie," Mormor said tenderly.

"I love you too, Mormor." And I meant it with my entire being. She had become the grandmother I had never had and for the past month, my sanity. I snuggled back down into my pillow and fell fast asleep.

That evening after supper my father came to visit with me. I could see the worry in his eyes and was thankful when Keane came walking in with a bouquet of wildflowers to help keep the conversation flowing and to help my father relax. "The flowers are lovely, thank you," I said, blushing as he set them in a vase on my bureau. He came and kissed my forehead and winked at me. That seemed to put a smile on my father's face. Keane sat on the edge of the bed as my father told us of his crops and coming harvest. He told us John and Celia had written from the Falls and were having a wonderful wedding trip. I saw Keane wince just a bit and wondered what he was thinking. Keane told my father of his dreams for his stables and all about Percheron horses.

My father sat in awe, living in Keane's dream as he spoke it. "That sounds like a wise investment, Son. We could use some good horse flesh available around these parts. I think you will do well, and the railway runs right through Crawford, making it easy for people to travel to you or to ship the animals," Father said, deep in thought. Keane looked so excited and boyish as he talked about his stables with my father. I couldn't help but hope he could pull his dreams off. I could see how happy he was just thinking of it.

My mother decided to stay another day with me, and Keane and Mormor set her up in the room next to mine. After my father left and my mother kissed me goodnight, Keane asked me if I wanted him to read to me. I doubted I could stay awake, but he seemed intent on doing so, so I gave in and let him. He sat in the rocking chair and began reading some of the Proverbs from the Bible. I do not know how long I slept, but when I awoke and needed to go to the washroom, I found Keane asleep in the rocking chair. I knew I had to have assistance although it pained me to admit it. "Keane," I whispered.

He immediately sat up straight. "What is it? What can I do for you?" he asked so tenderly, my heart raced. I could have kissed him.

I smiled weakly. "Could you get my mother for me? And then could you go to bed please. I want you to rest," I said softly.

He stood and kissed my forehead. "I will get your mother, but I will not leave," he said, walking away from me. Mother came in and helped me to the washroom. I bid her goodnight as Keane assured her he was staying near me. I sighed as I took in his tall form, so strong and muscular from all the farm work he did. He was lovely, and he looked very uncomfortable in the hard wooden rocking chair.

"Keane, please go to your bed. If you leave your door open, you can hear me when I call for you, or Mother can hear me. She is just next door. I will not get up alone; you have my word. But you must get some sleep," I insisted. He gave me a sleepy and rebellious smile that caused my heart to race, and he refused me. Oh, he was aggravating! I sighed and patted the bed next to me. "If you won't leave, then you might as well lie down here beside me. I cannot rest knowing you're sitting up all night," I said, trying my best to sound angry. His eyes searched mine. I thought he might refuse my bold offer, but he slid off his boots and lay on top of the blankets next to me. He lay on his back and looked up at the ceiling. I knew he was as nervous as I was. I reached over and took his hand in mine, and he smiled. I closed my eyes and fell fast asleep.

I continued to improve over the next several days although my energy was still slow to come. Robert came every morning to check on me. Mother and Mormor tried to stuff me full of beef every chance they had. My sisters came over and read to me or brought their sewing to work on as we visited. I still took several naps a day, but I was beginning to feel myself again. My mother returned home as she knew Keane stayed beside me each night. I was strong enough to walk to the washroom unassisted now even though, if Keane or Mormor was near, each felt it necessary to escort me to the door. Keane read the Bible to me every night until I fell asleep, and I found myself longing for the evenings to come so I could spend time with him. Sometimes he still seemed moody and distant, but he was still beside me and seemed to want my company.

The next morning when Robert came, he gave me a clean bill of health and told me I could slowly start doing light housework. I decided I needed to confide in him the depths of my feelings for Keane; it was not fair keeping him in suspense when, in my heart, I knew I couldn't leave my husband. "He may never love me, but my heart is tied to him. I made a vow to him, and I will not break it unless he asks me to," I said softly. Robert nodded in disappointment and perhaps a little anger. He quickly left. I felt terrible that I had hurt him and worried that now that I was well, Keane would go back to ignoring me. I realized I had fallen in love with Keane, and I had to see my marriage through. I would only seek an annulment if Keane asked me to.

"What are you doing?" I heard Keane ask, agitated, as I turned from the cook stove.

I smiled brightly despite his mood. "I am doing the baking," I said, happy to be of some use again.

He shook his head no. "It is too soon. You already cooked breakfast this morning, and this kitchen is as hot as Hades. Mormor can help, or I will send for Valynn. I want you to go lie on the sofa and rest," he said, taking my hands in his.

I pulled away and laughed. "The doctor released me for light house work, and I have two dozen cinnamon rolls nearly done rising. I cannot leave them," I insisted.

He pulled me closer, concern in his eyes. My stomach again made the tiny flutters at his nearness. "Mormor can watch them when she returns from her quilting bee," he said, trying to pull me gently into the parlor. I tried to pull away again with a chuckle, determined to finish my task as he was being unreasonable, but he brought me hard against his chest, his lips mere inches from mine, his blue eyes troubled. "I will not let you get sick again, Georgiana. You will do as I ask please," he said softly. I thought he might kiss me, hoped he would kiss me, but he swept me up into his arms and carried me toward the parlor. I could not help but wrap my arms tighter around his neck and lay my head against his chest, longing for his closeness. As he placed me down on the sofa, our eyes met and he gave me a mischievous grin, the one that melted my heart and caused my stomach to somersault deeply. "That was easy enough," he bragged.

I slapped his arm playfully. "I gave in just to get rid of you; don't you have work in the barn to do?" I asked coyly, surprising myself.

He frowned and then smiled. "No, don't believe I do. I do have cinnamon rolls to watch until Mormor arrives, though, so see you stay put on this sofa," he said, not letting me get the best of him. I growled in frustration as he left the room.

"Do you think you'd be up to a swim if we drove the buggy?" Keane asked a few days later.

I had cooked supper, Mormor had insisted on doing the dishes, and now I sat in the parlor, working on embroidering a pillowcase. It was only seven. I knew there was still a good two hours of daylight, and the hot August day had the entire house sweltering. "All right," I said, surprised he had offered.

It felt so good to get out of the house, and the water was cold and refreshing. I refrained from swinging from the rope but laughed as Keane plunged in. "It is good to hear your laugh again and see color in your cheeks," he said after a few minutes.

"I am as good as new," I said, smiling.

"I am thankful to God, I am," he said swimming away, but I couldn't help but smile at his sentiment. "I have heard it is harder to keep stubborn women down. I suppose I must be thankful you're so mule-headed," he teased. But I could see the sincerity in his eyes. I gasped and splashed water at him and pretended to be mad. Was I truly that stubborn? I repented in prayer as I swam around and watched the clouds above me. I always felt closer to God here, and to Keane.

I wore out much more quickly than usual, and Keane helped me from the water to the bank. I began to squeeze my hair out, but Keane took over for me and dried it awkwardly but tenderly with a towel. My heart raced at the close contact between us. "I will miss this place once harvest begins," Keane said as he lifted me into his arms to carry me back to the buggy.

Exhausted, I lay my head on his shoulder and hugged him tightly. "Me too," I whispered. Back at home he carried me up to my room and set me on the floor so I could change for the night. He sighed as if he wanted to say something important, but then he shut my door and left me alone.

He did not come and read the Bible with me that night, and I could not help but feel disappointed. I missed hearing his soothing voice reading the Word of God and him lying next to me, holding my hand in his until I fell asleep. I laid awake for hours before I closed my eyes and prayed fervently for wisdom. I wanted to do God's will, no matter the cost or sacrifice. If he meant me for Keane, I wanted to be there for him. I could no longer see Robert as part of my life's plan, and I prayed I had not deceived myself.

It was after midnight when I heard my bedroom door slowly open and saw Keane standing in the doorway. I quickly sat up. He came and sat beside me on the bed. "I am sorry to wake you," he said softly.

I shook my head. "I have not slept yet," I confided.

He sighed in relief. "Neither have I. I feel...I cannot hear you breathing in my room, so I lay and wonder if you're all right," he said tenderly.

"I am recovered, Keane. You do not have to worry so," I whispered.

He kissed my forehead. "I cannot help but worry," he confessed.

My heart raced at my boldness. I wrapped my arms around him, and he held me close. "Will you read to me?" I asked. He nodded, turned up the lamp, picked up the Bible, and then lay beside me. I lay my head against his shoulder as I listened to him read. I must have fallen asleep, but as he rose to leave me, I took his hand. "Please stay," I pleaded softly. He nodded and opened his arms as I snuggled against his chest and went back to sleep.

The next morning before it became too hot, Keane and Henry and I walked along the fields and barn yard as Keane described how he wanted to add onto the barn for the beginnings of his stable. He smiled as he mentioned sending for Gaspard after the harvest. I was thankful he was waiting until the crops were in and the money accounted for. I smiled excitedly as I pictured the mares with their foals prancing in the fields that would soon be set to pasture. I had never dreamt of living on a horse farm, and though I was a little frightened of horses at times, I was excited to be a part of the changes soon coming to Kenrick Farms.

After Keane took down the screen doors and shutters from the house, he and Henry sanded off the old peeling paint until the wood was nice and smooth. "What color do you want these painted, Mormor?" Keane asked, coming into the kitchen.

Mormor shrugged. "Well, they have been black for nearly thirty years. Ask Georgie. It is her house now; I want her to choose the color," she said, smiling.

I was rolling out a pie crust for a peach cobbler and looked up surprised. "I....I do not know what to say," I said, stunned and excited to have a choice in the say of what color to accent the beautiful farmhouse.

"Well, let me help you out. I have green paint, black paint, or a nice red paint," Keane said smiling. "If you want another color, you will have to wait and ride into town with me and see if Mr. Larkin has it in his store," he teased.

I smiled and thought of the various colors. "I like red," I said timidly, still loving my kitchen in the cheery red and white gingham. I could picture red rocking chairs leaning against the white farmhouse.

Keane smiled. "Good choice, red it is!"

"Red will be lovely, Georgie," Mormor agreed with a smile. I smiled as she turned back to her book. I had made my first decision in the new changes at Kenrick Farms, my new home.

Late that evening, as the sun was setting, Keane came into the house, calling me out to the front yard. We stood back together and looked at the new red shutters and decorative screen door, all in red. I clapped, happy with my choice and smiling from ear to ear. "I cannot believe it; it looks so beautiful," I said with tears in my eyes.

Keane hugged my shoulders. "This is your home now, Georgiana," he whispered tenderly.

I shook my head in disbelief. "I do not deserve it," I whispered. "It is too beautiful!"

"No one deserves Kenrick Farms more than you, Georgiana," he said, leaving me alone in the front yard. I wondered if he ever thought of Melody anymore and if perhaps he just had. It was the only explanation I could think of for his walking off and leaving me in such a tender moment. Or perhaps the moment was only special to me. I told myself not to feel hurt; this is what I had bargained for. It was now mine, and it was perfect, well, the house was anyway.

Keane avoided me the rest of the evening. I did not see him again until breakfast the next morning. "The house looks lovely, Keane. Thanks to you and Henry. I love the red; it is so fresh and inviting. I cannot wait for Mabel and the other ladies in my quilting bee to see it," Mormor said, smiling. I thanked Keane and Henry again as I set a large plate of biscuits and gravy in front of them.

"I say it's the least we can do for all these fine meals we have been partaking in," Henry said, smiling and giving me a wink. Keane remained quiet. Mormor watched him over her tea cup with a scowl. His moods seemed to change by the minute, and she could see it as plain as day. I excused myself to go and gather the laundry for washing.

I was in Henry's room in the barn, gathering his clothing and sheets, when I heard him and Keane come into the barn. "I have heard from my father back home; he has found a brood mare, a Percheron. She is located in Slatsville. I want to wire the owner and travel to look at her before harvest begins next week," Keane said, surprising me.

"I can watch things around here if you're worried about leaving," Henry assured Keane.

Keane thanked him and sighed. "I will travel alone. It is faster that way, and I do not want to leave Mormor in the house by herself." For some reason, I felt a little disappointed he didn't wish to take the trip with me.

Henry coughed. "Well, it might make a nice get away for you and Georgie; you never did take a honeymoon or nothing. I know Tobias would be happy to bring Mabel out for a few days to keep Ms. Addie company. And I'd be right here should they need me," Henry said. I had to smile at his trying.

"It's not like that with Georgiana and me. She will be happier here," Keane said with a frustrated sigh.

"Boy, you have the best woman in all of Lowe County as your wife, but you won't even try to love her," Henry said, disappointed, and then left the barn.

Tears filled my eyes as I leaned back against the wall until I heard Keane leave, or at least I thought he left. I left Henry's room and was leaving through the barn when Keane called out to me. "Georgiana, how long have you been in there?" Keane asked, startling me.

I grabbed my chest, startled, and turned away lest he see my disappointment. "Long enough," I said, sighing.

He frowned. "I haven't wired the owner yet; I do not know if I can arrange it before harvest or if it will need to wait," he said, sounding frustrated. I shrugged; since he had not consulted me on the matter, I would not act interested. I walked away toward the house and heard him curse softly as he kicked a bucket. I silently hoped he broke his toe.

Chapter Seven

A few evenings later, we were invited to my parents' house for dinner. It was to celebrate Celia's eighteenth birthday a few days late, but she and her husband had just returned from their two-week wedding trip. I dressed in my new yellow dress with the tiny white polka dots, and since Keane and Henry had been preparing for the harvest and were out in the barn, I had Mormor roll my hair into the rag curlers. Once my hair had dried, I gathered my thick curls to the side and tied it with a small yellow ribbon.

I made a light supper for Henry and Mormor, and when Keane came down stairs, he smiled appreciatively at my appearance. "You look beautiful, Georgiana!" he said softly. I thanked him, secretly cherishing his praise but wondering where it had been the past several days. I kissed Mormor's cheek goodnight.

"I cannot wait to see Celia," I said softly as Keane drove the buggy toward my parents' home.

Keane smiled. "I am certain she has missed you as well," he said, knowing how close my sisters and I were.

My parents greeted us warmly. "You are looking much better, Georgie," my father said, pleased, as he kissed my cheek.

"I feel better, Father," I assured him.

"Well, Keane, it appears you are taking good care of my daughter. Thank you," my father said, patting Keane's back warmly.

"I try my best, sir, but it isn't always easy; she is stubborn that daughter of yours," he said with a mischievous grin and a wink. I pretended to be shocked, enjoying seeing his handsome grin had returned. Then my sisters swarmed me, pulling me away to where Celia sat in the parlor.

"Happy birthday!" I said, hugging my sister who still glowed with her happiness.

"I have missed you so much, Georgie! Mother said you had taken ill. I am glad you are recovering," she said, hugging me tight.

"I am much better," I assured her. When Mother called us for dinner, Keane held out his hand to me, a silent plea not to leave him at the mercy of all my sisters who still thought he was the handsomest man in Crawford. I took his hand and squeezed it warmly in reassurance that he would survive. After my father led us in prayer, Celia and John told us of their wedding trip to the Falls, describing its beauty and the fun they had, as well as the sights they saw on the way.

I helped Mother serve the lemon cake and homemade ice cream and took my seat next to Keane as John told of receiving a letter from Matthias and Eleanor who had journeyed down to the shore for their wedding trip. "They are due back any day now; we will need Matthias for the harvest," John said. Keane and my father, along with Henry, would harvest my father's crops first, being the largest, and then Kenrick Farms next. The women would be cooking, canning, and doing barnyard chores.

Mother brought out a small wrapped gift for Celia, and we all admired the small jewelry box with the stained glass top. I had wrapped a peach cobbler in cheesecloth; Celia hugged me as if it were a better gift than the jewelry box.

"And now, we have a gift for all of you," John said, smiling. Celia stood up and cleared her throat.

"Come the end of next April, you will have your first grandbaby," she said, beaming with pride. Mother and Father gasped, and both began to cry tears of joy as we all congratulated John and Celia. I could not help but cry as I hugged my sister close, so happy for her. After only six weeks of marriage, Celia was expecting. My heart ached to know that I would never experience carrying a child in my womb, feeling it move inside of me. Keane's eyes met mine, a silent reminder present in their blue depths, reminding me that I had given up such things when I chose Kenrick Farms. I quickly looked away as I dried my tears and fought to keep my smile. I would not be envious; I would rejoice with Celia.

Keane was very quiet on the ride home. It was late, and as he helped me down from the buggy, his hands remained on my waist as he looked into my eyes. "That is some news from John and Celia, and so soon, isn't it?" he asked, his eyes never leaving mine.

I looked down to my feet and nodded. "Yes, I am very happy for them both. They have been in love for a year now, begging to marry for more than six months. It is more than I could have hoped for," I said, shivering for some reason.

"I wish...," Keane started, and then sighed, saying no more.

I gently took his hands from my waist and forced a smile. Kissing his cheek, I spoke softly. "Goodnight, Keane. Thank you for going with me," I said, and left him in the yard alone.

Three days before the harvest began, Mormor and I sat on the porch swing with our embroidery. The day was hot, but at least under the shade of the porch we could feel a gentle breeze. "I daresay September is just as hot as August this year," Mormor complained.

I nodded. "Just a few more weeks should bring cooler weather," I assured her. We saw Keane riding in from town, but he did not return my wave. Shortly we heard the back screen door slam and his heavy footfalls going up the stairs.

"I wonder what is wrong with Keane now?" I asked. Mormor looked concerned as well. We waited nearly an hour, but when I went in to start supper, he had yet to come down.

I placed the roast beef in the oven, went upstairs, and knocked on his bedroom door. He did not answer. "Keane," I called and slowly opened his door to find him sitting in a chair in the alcove, staring out the window. "Are you ill?" I asked softly. He shook his head no. "What is it? Did you get your train ticket to Slatsville?" I asked, knowing something was obviously wrong. He said nothing so I slowly walked toward him not knowing if I was welcome or not. I knelt before him and took his hand in mine. He wouldn't look at me. I sat on my knees before him holding his hand, content to sit in silence if he needed to.

"The letter is on the bed; you can read it," he said softly. I stood and took up the letter and sat on the side of his bed. After just a few minutes, I gasped, and tears filled my eyes. My heart hurt for Keane and his family and for myself as well. This proved he was still in love with Melody. "She betrayed me," he said softly. I knelt before him once again, wiping tears from my eyes. He looked at me confused. "Why are you crying?" he asked in a whisper.

"She hurt you," I whispered in return. I wanted to say, '*because no matter what I do, you still love her*'.

"But why would that make you cry?" he asked, leaning towards me and wiping my tears with his thumb.

"I do not want you to hurt," I whispered. "You love her, and she continues to hurt you, though she is hundreds of miles away."

He pulled me into his arms and held me close. "Oh Georgiana, is there anyone on earth as good as you? No, there is not," he whispered into my hair. I held him tightly; my heart breaking. "I am angry with her, but I just realized, after reading that letter, I no longer feel love for her," he whispered against my cheek. My heart nearly stopped at his words. "My pride feels betrayed, but mostly I hurt for Eitan and my family back home," he said sighing. I held him closer, and he tightened his embrace. "I never touched her in that way, and I am angry to think she tried to deceive me, and I am angry at my brother for thinking I was capable of doing such a thing. If Mormor and Grandfather had not insisted I marry you, I would be trapped raising another man's child," Keane whispered.

I pulled back from him. "But when you love someone so deeply, you would have loved her child, too. You would at least still have her, your dreams, your future," I said emotionally.

He shook his head. "She didn't really love me, and now I can see why she tried to pressure me to marry her so quickly. She would never have lived here on the farm. She could never take care of this place as you do," he said and shook his head. "I struggled letting go of someone whose only intent was to hurt me. Now, she will hurt my brother instead," he said angry.

"You cannot help that Eitan chose her. He knew she had once been yours, yet he chose her anyway. Yes, he was being deceived, but he made the choice himself. We must pray for them both; God can still work it out for them," I whispered, trying to ease his burden.

"Georgiana," he whispered. He pulled me to him and kissed me like he did that day in the barn so many weeks ago. My arms wrapped around his neck, and I kissed him back with everything I held in my heart for him. The screen door slammed downstairs, and Mormor was greeting someone inside the house so Keane broke our kiss. As I stood to leave, Keane pulled me back to him.

"I have never deserved you, my wife. But thank God he knew better than I what I needed," he whispered into my hair, making my heart skip a beat.

Harvesting began at my father's farm and I enjoyed being home once again, working alongside my mother and sisters. I did the baking and most of the cooking while my sisters did the hauling of water and barnyard chores. Mormor had come along. She sat in the parlor helping with mending and snapping the last of my mother's green beans to preserve.

Valynn and I walked out to the fields at noon to take the men their lunch and exchange the empty jug of water. Keane smiled and gave me a wink, and I couldn't help but feel proud that he was such a hard worker and had insisted on helping my father get his crops in safely first. I did not see Keane again until nearly dark when they brought the last wagon-load of wheat in for the day.

I had fried potatoes, ham, beans, and cornbread ready and had made a blackberry cobbler, peach cobbler, and a strawberry rhubarb pie. "Oh, I could kiss you, Wife," he teased as he bit into his favorite strawberry rhubarb pie. I blushed but silently wished he would kiss me. My mother and father both chuckled at my husband's humor, but Genevieve rolled her eyes at me. I couldn't help but savor my little sister's innocence. Soon enough she would be courting her own beau and facing so many of the struggles I found myself in.

We drove home with Henry and Mormor, and once the chores were done in the barn, I heard Keane ride away on his horse. I knew he went to the swimming hole to bathe. I fell asleep listening for his return.

The next day my three youngest sisters went to the fields with the men to help gather the cut wheat and bind it. I was left behind with Mother and Mormor to do the cooking. Keane and Father had insisted I not work in the fields this harvest. I was needed in the kitchen as they needed more pies. I knew it was all Keane's doing, for my father had expected me to help each year as always, but I knew Keane worried it was too soon after my illness. Although it kept me from seeing him most all day, I felt a little special that he worried over me so.

I helped Mother do her washing and hung the laundry to dry on the line in the back yard. At noon the wagon pulled up with my sisters and the men. I had steaks, gravy, potatoes, green beans, collard greens, and yeast rolls waiting, along with more pie. After dinner was cleared and the men back to the fields, we gathered and harvested the herbs from the garden, laying them out on newspapers to dry. Mormor labeled jars and helped with the dishes. She was very wise with herbs, and I listened carefully to her and Mother as they explained the process of drying and use for each herb. Some were for seasonings and some medicinal. Late that afternoon we picked the apples and peaches in the orchard. For dinner I had several apple pies made and two peach cobblers. I was so tired that night that I was asleep as soon as my head hit my pillow.

We spent one more day at my father's farm, and then my family's harvest was in. The next morning I rose early and made a large breakfast, for today the harvest at Kenrick Farms began. I had hardly seen Keane all week. This morning as he thanked me for breakfast and gave me a wink, I could hardly wait until the days slowed down once more in hopes we could spend more time together. I missed our playful bantering at the swimming hole and his reading to me when I had been ill. I found myself wondering if he missed me, too.

My sisters and I spent the morning making apple butter in the cheery red kitchen. It was a hot and tedious job. My arms ached from the stirring, but having my sisters with me and enjoying their conversations made it easier. I had missed them, missed the laughter and the teasing; sometimes it was too quiet in my new home.

At noon we walked out to the fields and took the men their lunch and fresh water. "You have a smart husband, Georgie. Kenrick Farms will double their crops next year, as well as having a new stable," Father said, smiling as he thanked me for the meal.

I smiled at Keane but couldn't help but shrug playfully. "Smart hmm? Haven't heard that about him before," I laughed.

Keane chuckled; he looked weary but never more handsome in my eyes. "When I am not so tired, I will get you back for that," he said, sighing. I laughed once again and reminded him not to dare a farm girl; I was still saving the manure pile as an option for repayment.

That night I awoke, startled, and fear crept up my spine. I looked beside me to see that Keane had never joined me in my room. He hadn't for over a week, but somehow I suppose I had hoped he would be there. My room lit up as I looked out my window and held my breath. It was storming, with lightening flashing too closely, and large hail fell to the ground below my window. I began to pray over the rest of our crops, asking God to protect them. While I was thankful that my garden was up and preserved in the cellar, along with canned apples, canned peaches, blackberry preserves, and tons of apple butter, we needed this last wheat crop for cash money to see us through until the next spring, especially if Keane was to start his stables and the breeding of the Percheron horses. Goose pimples covered my arms as I watched the fierce storm rage outside.

Suddenly a strong wind struck the side of the house; I heard my window popping. Screaming, I stepped back just in time as glass shattered and blew into my room. The screen door slammed downstairs, and I heard Keane yelling, "Mormor, Georgiana, get in the cellar." I heard him open Mormor's door and yell frantically up to me. I had held my arms in front of my face when the glass blew in, but I could feel shards on my night dress and in my hair as I made my way into the hall. Keane was already at the top of the stairs and reached for my hand, practically dragging me down with him. "Are you all right?" he asked, rushing me.

"Yes, but what is it?" I asked, frantically. The screen door had blown open and rain and hail blew up onto the sleeping porch as Keane lifted me into his arms and ran to the side of the house where the cellar was. Henry helped me down the dark steps as Keane slammed the door closed and bolted it. Henry lit a lantern, and Mormor gasped as she tried her best to pull shards of glass out of my long hair. Keane took his shirt off, using it as a rag, and began brushing the shards from my nightdress and arms.

We heard the wind roaring outside. I shivered in fright. Keane pulled me into his arms and kissed my forehead. "Thank God we are all right," he said. We all agreed.

"I pray my family is all right," I said into Keane's shoulder. Keane led us in prayer for my family and for the other farms lying just past ours.

Nothing could describe the fear I felt when Keane led us out of the cellar. I looked around at the destruction and could not hold back my sobs. Half the barn was gone, several fruit trees uprooted, limbs laying all over the yard, and large patches of dirt and earth where our wheat crop had been just half an hour ago. Keane held me close to one side, his Mormor on the other, as we stood with Henry and took in the damage. "God will provide," Mormor said confidently.

I knew He would. God had always been faithful, but my heart still ached. "My family," I whispered.

"Henry and I will ride over," Keane said, looking to make certain the horses were still there. One horse was at least.

"I had best round up the livestock," Henry said, leaving us. The chickens were squawking. Mormor and I rushed to gather them, but it was nearly impossible seeing how they were spooked.

Keane rode over to my parents' farm and was soon back. "They are all well. The storm came up from behind them; they lost the large work shed and perhaps a wagon, but the barn and house are all just fine," Keane said smiling.

I thanked God, and Mormor hugged me closely. "The Lord gave and the Lord hath taken away, blessed be the name of the Lord," Mormor said emotionally.

The sun was fully up now as I went upstairs to dress. I sighed as I found my floor full of water and glass. I stripped the wet bedding and swept up the water and glass. Keane came up and helped me take the mattress outside to dry, and then he nailed an oil skin over the window until a glass could be purchased. I moved my things into the bedroom at the end of the hall, liking that its window did not face the Southwest where all the heavy storms had come from.

"Georgie!" I heard someone call upstairs, and smiled as I rushed downstairs to find Celia and Eleanor. I hugged them both, thankful they had come. They hurried to help me clean the water that had been brought in all over the kitchen floor.

I quickly put on tea and coffee as I realized we had more guests. John and Matthias were outside talking to Mormor and Keane. "Oh my, we haven't had breakfast," I said, rushing to make a large meal. Celia quickly helped me, but Eleanor looked weak and green tinted as she sat at the table sipping her tea.

"We were lucky. Just a few trees down was all, but Mille and Drew lost their house," Celia said sadly.

"Are they all right?" I asked, gasping.

Celia nodded. "Drew heard the wind and got Millie down into the cellar just in time. John and Matthias are planning their house raising immediately, and it looks like a barn raising at Kenrick Farms next," she said, hugging me closely to comfort me.

"We have plenty of room here. Will you tell Millie she and Drew are welcome to come here and stay?" We had four empty bedrooms available.

"How nice of you, Georgie. I am certain they will appreciate it," Eleanor said.

"Eleanor, are you well?" I asked concerned. She was never this quiet. She blushed, and suddenly I knew. I hugged her closely and she looked surprised. "I am so happy for you and Matthias," I said sincerely.

Her eyes filled with tears. "Oh Georgie, but if only you could be so happy," she said, worried for me.

I smiled. "I am content. Things are much better between Keane and me. We are friends," I said.

"Friends, just friends? That is so sad," she said, covering her face and weeping.

Celia rubbed my back gently. "It is all right, Georgie, poor Ellie has cried for a week now. Dr. Anderson said it's just her body changing with the baby," Celia said tenderly.

"Have you cried like that?' I asked my sister, concerned.

Eleanor frowned. "No, Celia has not been sick, tired, or weepy. Just me, and I am having all three symptoms," she said, drying her eyes. Celia grinned and shrugged.

When Keane came inside, I pulled him into the parlor to ask if Drew and Mille could stay with us. He sighed and nodded. "If you would rather they not, I understand," I said softly.

"No, it is the Christian thing to do. I just worry....about sleeping arrangements," he said. I understood. He didn't want them to see we didn't share a room.

"They could have the guestroom off the parlor," I suggested.

"Yes, that would work. We can store whatever they have left of their belongings in one of the empty rooms upstairs." He kissed my forehead, and needing reassurance or comfort, which one I didn't know, I nearly jumped on him with my arms going around his neck. He held me closely.

"Will we make it?" I asked, worried about the crops.

"Do not worry; I will take care of you," he promised. "Thank God I listened to you and we prayed about the timing of bringing Gaspard and building the stable. It would all have been gone, just like that," he whispered.

I kissed his cheek and looked up into his eyes. "It will happen, in God's timing, Keane; you will have your stables. I have been praying for God to give you your heart's desires," I whispered. To my surprise, he grabbed me fiercely against him and thanked me, holding me tightly until Eleanor called for me.

Later that afternoon Keane came to me. "We will need to move Henry into the house. The barn is too unstable now. It will need to be torn down and rebuilt. It is not safe for him until then," he said concerned. I nodded. We were about to have a house full.

Mormor came to join us. "I have worked this all out in my head," she assured us. "I will take the guest room off the parlor; we will let Drew and Mille use my room. It is much too big for just me alone, and this will give them privacy. You and Keane can keep your rooms and Henry can take one of the empty rooms upstairs," Mormor said decisively. And so that evening Kenrick Farms grew from three people living in the old farmhouse to six.

There were several farms hit hard by the storm, so rebuilding began immediately. Keane and Drew would leave early in the morning and ride to whichever farm was hosting a barn or house raising, and Millie, Mormor and I cooked. We would meet up with the other women at the raisings to feed the men. It was heartwarming to see our small community gathering together to build someone a new house or a new barn. Some folks like Drew and Millie had lost nearly everything. I shared two of my new dresses with Millie, and Celia and Eleanor shared a few of theirs as well. When we weren't cooking, we were sewing clothing or blankets for those who needed them or salvaging what was left of the fall garden.

Keane and I didn't have much time alone, not that we ever had shared much time together, but my loneliness subsided as the house was now full of laughter every evening. We would play card games in the kitchen after chores or play music in the parlor. Henry could play the harmonica and often joined me as I sang and played the piano. Keane had not returned to my room for many weeks although I lay and listened to his footsteps in the hallway, each night, pausing outside my door as if he wanted to come in. But then he would turn and go back into his room. I missed his reading to me and falling asleep to the sound of his voice, holding his hand in mine. I hated that instead of life's trials drawing us closer together, he seemed even more determined to keep his distance.

It had been nearly two weeks since the storm, and I had the windows open letting the cool breeze drift in and refresh the house. It was nearly October, and the air was a little cooler now, especially at night. I stood in the kitchen making pies as the next day would be our barn raising. Drew and Millie's house was nearly finished, and soon they would be moving in. I would miss our friends. Their liveliness and laughter helped ease my loneliness.

Millie was outside butchering a chicken for dinner, when I saw her out the kitchen window, heaving behind the garden. I sighed and then smiled. I poured a cool cup of well water into a glass and went outside to find her. She lay in the grass moaning as I helped her to sit up. "Drink this," I said smiling. She blushed and sipped the cool water. "How long have you known?" I asked her, brushing back a strand of black hair from her eyes.

"I am just now suspecting. I missed my time a few weeks back, and now this," she said blushing again. I helped her to stand and wash up in the kitchen. I made her a cup of peppermint tea and ordered her to rest in bed.

Mormor hugged me closely as I resumed my baking. "Perhaps one day it will be you," she said tenderly.

I smiled and shook my head no. "It doesn't matter. I will be so busy helping those three with their babies, sewing and baking. Mother just told me Isaac Stein has asked my father's permission to start courting Valynn next month when she turns seventeen. I will be plenty busy," I assured her but knew she could see right through me.

When Drew and Keane returned home that evening and Drew found out Millie was in bed sick, he sent Henry for Dr. Childers despite our protests. Mormor and I sat on the front porch just as Dr. Childers and Dr. Anderson arrived. Robert greeted me coolly; I regretted that he had not forgiven me yet. What was worse was the fear that perhaps I had once again missed God's will. Had Robert been God's way of fixing my mess with Keane? I sighed and could no longer question myself; I was in love with my husband for better or for worse.

Keane had just joined us on the porch when Drew came running out whooping and hollering excitedly. I smiled through tears of joy as he picked me up and swung me around and kissed Mormor's cheek. "I am going to be a father!" he kept saying over and over. He walked the doctors to their horses, thanking them the entire way.

Mormor and I couldn't help but giggle as we watched him. "Poor Millie, it will be a long seven and a half months with Drew this excited," I said, going back into the house to finish my chores for the evening. With everyone fed and occupied, I decided to take a walk and clear my head. It had been hard to find time for my own thoughts with a house full of people.

I decided to walk down to the swimming hole to see how it fared after the storm. As I walked, I passed remnants of the damaged wheat here and there and prayed God would see us through the winter months. I had already thought of ways I could earn money to help us financially by selling my pies and cobblers in town and perhaps taking in wash and mending. I had watched my parents over the years, facing these life trials, never faltering in their faith. But now that it was happening to me, to my family, I felt myself worrying, and knew I had to surrender these worries to God. I had to keep my faith and trust in God's provision, just as Mormor and my parents had their entire lives.

It was a beautiful evening as I found the swimming hole untouched by the storm. I smiled thinking of the times Keane and I had come to swim. The day he had thrown me into the water, the day he made fun of the towel in my hair, and the day he had kissed me so passionately in the barn and again in his room. Such silly little things, but they were all I had of him.

I quickly pulled off my shoes and stockings and tucked my skirt into the belt at my waist and waded in. It was very cold, perhaps too cold, but it was refreshing. I smiled as I saw the rope hanging above me in the tree and closed my eyes, remembering the times we had swung out into the deep, peals of laughter echoing across the water. I missed Keane. He still lived in the same house with me, our rooms next door to one another, yet we hardly spoke, and never touched.

I allowed my tears to flow freely and soon my body wracked hard with sobs that sent me to the bank on my knees. I needed this time alone, this cleansing cry, this surrendering of my desires to God, and taking what He would give me instead. I lay on my back, my feet dangling in the stream, and prayed for strength to endure, for peace in my heart and for blessings on my marriage, until I must have fallen asleep.

CHAPTER EIGHT

"Georgiana! Dear God, no! Georgiana!" I heard, as someone shook me in the dark.

I gasped. I was so cold. I quickly realized my feet were in water and pulled them out. "Keane, where am I?" I asked, afraid and trying to remember where I was. I was in his arms in seconds.

He sat on the ground and held me close, rocking me like a child as his kisses covered my face. "Are you all right? Are you hurt?" he asked, trying to search me with the dim lantern light.

"I am fine, just cold," I said shivering. He helped me put my shoes back on, swearing under his breath when he felt how cold my feet were. "I came for a walk and the water felt so good," I stammered.

"Well, now you'll be lucky not to catch your death in cold," he said, lifting me into his arms and carrying me to his horse. "Everyone has been worried sick about you. Millie is distraught, thinking you ran off because of her and the….," he stopped talking then and hugged me to his chest.

"I did not run off; I merely went for a walk, and I must have fallen asleep after wading," I insisted.

He lifted my chin up with one hand. "Even in this dim light I can see you've been crying," he said, shaking his head.

"Oh, goodness! I do not want them to see I have been crying!" I said, putting my cold hands on my face to relieve some of the redness. I pushed off the horse and rushed back to the stream and began to splash my face with the cool water.

"Stop it! Georgiana, you are cold enough. Let's get you home." He lifted me back into his arms and put me on the front of his horse. I felt embarrassed as we rode home slowly. How could I have fallen asleep out here, with my feet in the water? It had been so quiet and peaceful; my cry had been so releasing and cleansing. I suppose my body had simply found rest. Now my husband was quite annoyed by it. I still felt very tired, and without thinking, I leaned back against Keane's chest and turned my head against his warm neck. He always smelled so wonderful. I couldn't help but sniff him again and smiled, missing his closeness. He seemed edgy all of a sudden. "Georgiana, what are you doing to me?" I heard him whisper against my hair.

"You always smell so good," I said softly against his skin. Suddenly the horse stopped, the lantern dropped, and his lips were against mine in a passionate kiss. His hands were in my hair, and I was dizzy with love for this man. Suddenly realizing he needed the lantern light to help us get home, he released me and slid from the horse, picking up the lantern. He rubbed his free hand across his face in what seemed to be frustration. My heart still raced from his unexpected kiss as he walked in front of the horse, leading her home. I didn't know if I had scared him or repulsed him, but he was not climbing back on the horse. He was keeping his distance. I found myself again wondering why I wasn't enough for Keane and wondering what more I could do to reach him.

I had a lot of explaining to do as I found a kitchen full of worried friends and family. I assured Millie I was more than thrilled about her baby and that I would miss her and Drew once they moved home that coming weekend. Keane had me soak my cold feet in a pan of hot water and Mormor made me a cup of chamomile tea.

When Drew and Millie retired for the night, Mormor said she needed to speak with us. We still sat at the kitchen table, and I thought it strange Henry stayed. I swallowed hard; were we going to lose the farm since most of our crops were destroyed? "There is only one way to say this, plain and simple, but first know a lot of thought and prayer has gone into this decision. And the decision is made," she said smiling now. "Henry has asked me to marry him, and today, I said yes."

Keane and my mouths dropped to the table in shock. Keane looked to Henry who now held Mormor's hand tenderly; it was plain to see the affection between them. "What about Grandfather?" Keane asked in shock.

"I will always love your grandfather. Henry loved him, too, but he is in heaven, and he would want me to be happy, to go on with my life," she assured Keane.

I reached over and hugged her warmly, tears in my eyes. "I wish you both many years of love and happiness," I said, smiling.

"Thank you, Georgie. I knew you would understand and be happy for us," she said relieved.

"I wish you both joy," Keane said softly.

Mormor smiled. "The reason we told you tonight is, we do not wish to build Henry on a room in the barn. We want you to expand the barn and include the stables you will need for your breeding business, Keane. We would like to retire, and move into town, perhaps do some traveling," she said, smiling at Henry.

"Move to town!" I exclaimed.

"Mormor, we have more than enough room for you both in the house. There is no need to move. You can both retire but live here with us," Keane said, almost pleading.

"We would like to be alone, surely you understand. But, I suppose if Henry would like to, we could build a small house out back, perhaps behind the orchard," Mormor said, looking to Henry.

"I would like that," he said, kissing her hand tenderly. I climbed the stairs to my room feeling as if I had lost the last thing that held me to Kenrick Farms, Mormor.

It was just after midnight when I heard my door creak open. Turning to find Keane standing in the doorway, I sat up in bed. "Are you asleep?" he asked softly.

I shook my head no. He closed the door softly behind him and came to sit beside me on the bed. "I suppose my late nap is keeping me awake," I confessed.

He sighed. "This entire thing with Mormor and Henry is keeping me awake," he said, lying down beside me as if he meant to stay.

I lay my head against his shoulder and took his hand in mine. "Are you not happy for Mormor?" I asked softly.

"I do not know. I know I should be, but it is hard to see her holding Henry's hand," he said honestly.

"Jorik would want her to be happy. She is very much in love again. That is all any woman wishes for, is love," I said without thinking.

"Is that what you wish for, Georgiana? Do you wish for love?" he asked in a whisper. I moved away from him; I felt as if he was mocking me, knowing it was something I would never have. "Hey, what is it? What is wrong?' he asked surprised, grabbing my arm before I could leave the bed.

"It doesn't matter what I wish for, but please do not mock me," I said without looking at him.

He pulled me back against him, his arm going around my waist, his cheek against mine. "I am not mocking you. I long to know what it is that you wish for." My eyes filled with tears. For over two months I had fought for what I thought I wanted and against what I couldn't have. "Georgiana," he whispered, turning my face towards his.

"I just want….I want to be enough," I said, turning away from him again and laying my face against my pillow.

Keane kept his arms tight around me, holding me. "You are a great deal more than enough, Georgiana." I lay there wondering how he could say that; how his words did not match his actions. How those nights he feared losing me, he stayed by my side, only to leave me alone at night once I was well. How could he hold me and kiss me passionately one minute but then not kiss me or hold my hand for weeks again. I wasn't enough. I sat up in bed quickly.

"What is it, Georgiana?" he asked.

"Keane, if Mormor marries Henry, then what becomes of us? Does that void the farm and marriage agreement that she and Jorik ordered?" I asked with my mind whirling.

Keane took my hands in his. "Nothing will change, Georgiana."

I shook my head wildly. "It may void it, and then you could be free….you could buy me out as you wished, go on with your life," I said, trying to reason with him.

He looked at me with utter surprise. "Do you truly want that now?" he asked.

"I only want your happiness, Keane. It is more important to me than my share of the farm, and for over two months now, you have been miserable. This could be your chance at happiness," I said honestly.

"I do not want things to change, Georgiana. Besides, with that failed wheat crop, I could never borrow the money to pay you, even if you wanted me to," he said frustrated. I lay down beside him but turned the other way. "And, I haven't been miserable these past two months, not entirely. I asked you for patience while I worked through all these feelings," he said softly.

"I just want to help you," I whispered, needing things to change between us somehow. I couldn't stand this any longer, going from moment to moment wondering how he felt.

"Then please, let me hold you," he whispered back. I snuggled into his chest and lay awake long after he fell asleep.

The next morning we rushed getting everything ready for the barn raising. I was anxious to see how the new barn and stables would look as well as the small house for Henry and Mormor. At the breakfast table Keane, Henry, and Mormor sat drawing out plans for the small house, barn, and stable. "Oh, we do not need that much room," Mormor said as Keane drew the simple plan.

I stood with my coffee, frowning, not happy at all that Mormor was leaving us. "What is that frown for, Georgie?" Henry asked with a tender smile.

"I suppose it just seems strange that this big house sits empty while you build another," I said, not wanting Mormor to move out. She was my sunshine and the only one who greeted me with love at Kenrick Farms.

"Georgiana, Henry suggests we put in a wood floor in the barn, like the Stein's, for dancing. What do you think?" Keane asked softly. I looked surprised.

"We could host parties and church socials," he added, watching me intensely.

I shrugged. "It seems very expensive. Perhaps just focus on the stables you are going to need instead," I said concerned. I knew Keane had said he would never be able to get a loan without the crop.

"Do not worry about the money, Georgie," Mormor said tenderly.

Millie and Drew came in from outside, and Keane asked Drew his opinion on the barn layout and the wood floor. Drew smiled his approval. "Well, my wife loves to dance, so I will make the decision. Kenrick Farms will have the finest barn dancing floor this county has seen," Keane said, smiling and giving me a wink.

"Oh, Georgie, how wonderful!" Millie exclaimed excitedly. I tried to thank Keane, but I couldn't help but worry it would cost too much. Did Keane know how to manage money and save for emergencies? What about the horses? I soon realized I had no idea where we stood financially.

When everyone headed out to the barn yard, I took Keane's hand and pulled him into the parlor. "I am worried. We lost most of the wheat crop. We lost the barn. Now you're planning to enlarge it with stables and add a dance floor just for me. I would rather you focus on the horses and barn. It is a thoughtful gesture, but I do not need such a fancy gift. I have already spoken with Mr. Larkin, and he said he would be more than happy to sell my pies and breads in his store. It will allow me to help out financially in some way," I said, noticing the scowl on Keane's face.

"Georgiana, I have a bit of savings put back for the stables and horses. Mormor wants to gift us the rest we need for the barn. Grandfather had a nice savings put back, and she and Henry insist on our building this barn and stable. I plan on paying them back out of the proceeds of the first foal. And nothing is too good for *my wife*. You have given up so much, received nothing in return but a hard time. Let me give you this dance floor. Everyone in town will enjoy it. And as for you working and selling your baked goods, I have to say no. If something happens and we need the extra money, I will allow you to, only because I know everyone will be fighting to buy your pies. But I am the husband; I am to provide and take care of *my wife*, and I will. Just give me a chance," he pleaded almost frustrated.

I nodded. It was his pride talking, but I knew from watching my father how important it is to a man's confidence to prove to be a good provider. "I trust you," I said, kissing his cheek.

He quickly kissed my lips and smiled. "Let's go build our dreams, W*ife*," he said, smiling and causing my heart to ache inside with love for him. I nodded and followed him outside. He had said 'our dreams'; did he have any idea how much that meant to me?

The town folk began to arrive, my parents and sisters included. Women got to work setting out tables and benches for seating while Keane and Henry showed the men the plan for the layout of the new barn and stables. After Pastor Crawley said a blessing and asked for protection over the men, the work began. I was excited to see Celia and Eleanor, and soon all five of us sisters were together again. We shared recipes in my kitchen and talked of the latest fashions and the new fall hats in the Larkin's Mercantile window. Mormor had her group of friends sitting with her in the parlor. They worked on their mending or embroidery while they visited. Valynn hung close to Eleanor and Celia knowing she was to be the next Stein bride in a year's time. Millie shared her news of expecting, and suddenly the three brides were talking of nothing but sewing baby clothes and baby blankets. I quickly went outside to set up the wash tubs for the men to use before dinner.

At noon we rang the dinner bell and stood behind the lines of tables as the men filled their plates. "Keane, which one of these is Georgie's pie?" John asked with a grin.

Keane pointed to four different pies and smiled. "But the strawberry rhubarb is all mine, Boys." he said teasing.

"Your wife makes the best pies," Drew said softly, so Millie didn't hear.

I couldn't help but smile, and Keane gave me a wink. "Yes, she does. I am a lucky man," Keane said, smiling proudly. My stomach fluttered, and I hurried to help my mother carry out another pan of fried chicken.

By the end of the day the barn and stables were framed and the stairs and loft put in. Tomorrow they would finish putting on the outside boards, then would roof and frame Henry and Mormor's future house.

Keane held my hand as he walked me through the layout of the new barn, showing me where everything would be. He would build the stalls in the backside of the barn that would serve as the stables, as not to take away from the large open floor. "What color should we paint it?" he asked me with a proud smile. I smiled and shrugged. "I like red barns," he said thoughtfully.

I smiled. "Then red it is. It will complement the shutters on the house, and everything will match so nicely."

"But what if you liked blue?" he asked, with that mischievous grin.

I laughed. "I do like blue but not on a big barn in my back yard."

"I like blue, too. The blue of your eyes match the blue flowers in your wedding dress," he said, catching me off guard. I was surprised he remembered what I wore to our wedding. I blushed, and he pulled me closer. "Do you remember the last time we stood in a barn together?" he asked softly, his eyes searching mine. I swallowed hard and nodded. Then I boldly reached up on my tip-toes and kissed him on the mouth and took off running for the house.

"Wait! Where are you going?" he asked as I laughed.

"I am not going back in that horse trough," I said, still running. I heard his footfalls behind me as I reached the back door, only to have it shut in my face and locked. I looked up surprised to see Millie, Drew, and Mormor on the other side, smiling. I gasped, shocked that they would lock me out. Keane was about to catch me. I shook the door handle and squealed for them to let me in. They smiled and all shook their heads no. I squealed with laughter as Keane reached the back porch; I jumped from the side and took off running for the front of the house, but I heard the front door close and lock before I reached the front porch. "You all will pay for this!" I yelled at them as I kept running toward the fields, hoping Keane was too tired to chase me. I found a patch of damaged wheat and squatted down low behind it, hiding, listening for his foot falls.

"Come out, Georgiana. You owe me something," I heard him call, teasing as he reached the field. I smiled but kept crouched low. I had always been an excellent hider playing with my sisters in our own wheat fields. I saw him go the opposite direction through the fields; I sighed in relief as I sat on the ground to catch my breath. Suddenly, something jumped from behind me and my back hit the ground hard. Keane landed on me and rolled me to my side, knocking the wind out of me. "Oh gosh, Georgiana, I was just playing. I truly didn't mean to hurt you," he said, trying not to laugh as I struggled to catch my breath. He helped me sit up and patted my back until I sucked in air. "You aren't wearing that blasted corset again are you?" he teased. I feigned shock and pushed him on his backside and tried to run away from him again, but he pulled me to his lap, laughing with me. "You owe me something," he whispered.

I could feel his heart racing. I smiled. "How do you get that?" I asked. My head was reeling from being in his lap.

"You owe me a kiss, for tempting me with that little peck back in the barn and then running off to leave me alone," he said, holding my face in his hands.

"You asked me what we did, so I showed you, but I will not end up in the horse trough again, Keane Kenrick," I whispered, breathless.

"Kiss me again, Georgiana," he whispered. He pulled me closer to his chest, and I boldly kissed him. "You are so beautiful," he said, pressing his forehead to mine.

I could hardly believe his actions toward me, calling me beautiful. I felt so afraid. It was an excited fear, and I longed for him to hold me. "Keane, please hold me," I pleaded softly.

He smiled and kissed me until I was certain I would faint. He laid me next to his side in the wheat with his arms around me. He held me as we watched the sky above us turning colors of the late evening. "This is all ours, Georgiana, all ours, my beautiful wife." I had no idea what had changed in my husband's heart, but my own heart soared to the clouds above as I silently thanked God for listening to my prayers.

The next day the barn roof was put on, and the sides went up. It was a large barn with the stables on the back side. Even without paint, it looked magnificent. I swept the barn floor clean as the men moved to the orchard to frame up Henry and Mormor's cottage. After dinner tonight there would be dancing. I never imagined it would be in *my* new barn, at *my* new home, at Kenrick Farms. A few chairs and tables were moved to the sides of the new barn and the musicians set up where the stalls would eventually be. I carried out numerous jugs of sweet tea and water while Celia and Valynn covered the tables with the gingham tablecloths.

After everyone finished eating, the dancing started. Eleanor, Valynn, Millie, Celia, and I visited as we watched the community come together and celebrate their hard work. Henry and Mormor danced by. I declared she looked ten years younger since she had told us she was to marry. John claimed Celia and his younger brother Isaac claimed Valynn, leaving Eleanor, Millie, and me.

"Georgie, would you do an old friend a favor and dance with him?" I heard and looked to find Robert standing next to me, his hand held out for mine.

I looked around but didn't see Keane anywhere. I felt I needed his approval first but knew it would be rude to turn Robert down, so I nodded and smiled, thanking him. As we began to waltz, I spoke. "I thought you might never forgive me," I said softly.

He smiled, but it was still a hurtful smile. "I could never.... not forgive you, Georgie. You're one of those people no one can hate, even when you break his heart," he said, smiling gently. It did not make me feel much better. "I pray your marriage is progressing and you are happy."

I nodded. "I am happy," I said assuring him.

"Then that is all I can wish for. Still friends?" he asked softly.

I nodded and smiled. We spoke no more and as the song ended, warm hands came around my waist. "Can I have my wife for the next dance, Dr. Anderson?" Keane asked. I held my breath, dreading what might come, but Robert graciously bowed away. Keane swept me into his arms onto the dance floor, his eyes searching mine. "So the good doctor got the first dance in my new barn with my bride?" Keane asked, irritated.

I frowned. "I didn't see you anywhere; I was going to ask if you minded," I said, getting irritated myself. "Why are you so jealous of Robert?" I asked softly.

"Because I know you cared for him. I have heard how you nearly courted. And he looks at you with longing. I know he would take you away from me in a heartbeat if you said the word," he said with something similar to fear in his eyes.

"But why argue with him so much? The decision lies in my hands, and I am not going to leave you," I said tenderly.

He pulled me a little closer and sighed. "I am sorry. It just makes me angry to see you in his arms," he said honestly.

"And it most likely hurts him to see me in yours, especially after I chose you," I said, and gasped, realizing what I had let slip.

Keane looked furious. "What do you mean, chose me?" he
asked.

I shook my head. "It isn't the time or place, Keane. Please let
us enjoy the party," I pleaded. But he led me calmly, but firmly,
outside and to the house and up the stairs. "Keane, we cannot
leave our guests," I said softly.

"Tell me what you meant, Georgiana, *you chose me*," he said,
crossing his arms.

Now I was angry as well. "You make it sound so terrible,
Keane. Forgive me for not knowing you didn't wish for me to
choose you!" I shouted.

"I didn't say that. Now answer me," he demanded.

I swallowed hard and sighed. "When I was hurt and Robert
came, he let me know he wanted me to be happy; he felt
perhaps the lack of love or affection might be the cause of my
suffering. He said we could annul our marriage easily since it
was in name only, and he would then marry me and take me
away from the gossip. Then I could give you your greatest
desire, the farm, and he would provide for me, give me
children, affection. I told him no, I couldn't leave you. He
wanted me to think about it, but I couldn't. I wouldn't. I made
vows before God. I told him when he asked me again weeks
later that I could never leave you. I care too much," I said with
tears streaming down my cheeks. Why was Keane so angry with
me?

"He would give you children, affection, and you still turned
him down?" he asked, softly shaking his head in disbelief.

I nodded. "He meant nothing bad toward you, Keane. He just
couldn't stand to see me unloved and stuck in a loveless
marriage. Tonight he merely wanted us to be friends again,

with no hard feelings. He knows my heart is here at Kenrick Farms.... and with you," I said, sitting on my bed feeling defeated and confused.

Keane knelt before me and lifted my chin in his hand. "You are not unloved, Georgiana....I feel so much for you....I want to give you everything your heart desires," he said, kissing me passionately. The door slammed downstairs, and we could hear voices looking for kitchen utensils.

"We'd best head back out there," I said softly, but wishing he would have said more. He felt so much of what for me?

Keane nodded and stood. "You know, I might not mind having an empty house for a time," he said with a sigh. I blushed at his meaning and took his arm as we returned to try and enjoy the dancing and what remained of our guests.

Saturday came, and we all helped Drew and Millie move into their new house. It was a lovely farmhouse, not as large as Kenrick Farms, but much newer. Millie was bubbly and excited as she directed us where to put things. People in town had donated furnishings. Keane and I gave them one of the extra bedroom sets from upstairs, intending to turn the room into Keane's study. We ate dinner in town at the diner and picked up supplies before heading home. "Oh my!" Mormor said as she read a letter that had been waiting on her at the mercantile.

"Is something wrong, Mormor?" I asked, concerned.

She bit her lip with a puzzled look on her face. "I think it might be," she said. I looked at her confused. "Keane, your parents are coming next week for my wedding," she said, watching for his reaction.

He smiled and nodded. "Good, I can't wait for them to meet my wife and to see our farm," he said happily.

"Well, they are not coming alone. Your bother Ian and his wife Caterina are joining them.... and Eitan and Melody," she said, holding her breath.

I gasped and looked to Keane, but he only nodded. "That is good. I have not seen my brothers in many months. It is unfortunate Eitan brings Melody, but he is the one stuck with her, not me, thank heavens," he said, surprising us with a smile. I was glad to see Keane was not worried about Melody coming; however, I was quite bothered by this news.

The barn had two coats of red paint, and it was beautiful, especially in the evening as the sun was setting. Keane and I sat on the fence rail and simply admired what was to be the beginning of Keane's dreams of raising Percheron horses. Keane telegraphed his father. They would escort Gaspard to his new home, Kenrick Farms, as they traveled to join us for Mormor and Henry's wedding. Keane worked night and day building the stalls and the grain shoots. I knew he was itching to leave for Slatsville to see about the new brood mare, but he had yet to plan his trip. I again prayed for God's wisdom and timing for Keane and these important decisions being made.

With guests arriving in mere days, I stood in the hallway upstairs once again trying to decide where to place everyone. Henry worked hard on the cottage in the orchard and said he would move his things out that evening which freed one room. I needed three, and we had just given one of the extra beds to Drew and Millie. Keane stood listening, trying to help me. "I can solve this entire problem," Mormor said smiling. We looked at her surprised. We had been discussing this for three days and had gotten nowhere. "Keane, I am certain you do not want your brothers knowing you insist on separate rooms with your bride. So temporarily, let us move you and Georgie into mine and Jorik's old room. It is the largest and, of course, is the room expected to be the suite for the owners. We will move the bed and dresser from the guest room off the parlor upstairs to the empty bedroom. The guest room off the parlor becomes your study, as it should be. We will move the desk out of the parlor into the new study, making more room for chairs for our guests. That puts me sleeping upstairs but only for a few nights and then we will have three other rooms as needed once you and Georgie move downstairs," she said. My mouth opened in surprise; my problem was solved.

Keane smiled. "Mormor, you amaze me. We have been struggling with this for days and you just now speak up!" he said, hugging her. She winked at me mischievously once Keane walked away. I blushed, suddenly realizing what she had done. Now Keane and I would share a room and a bed for an entire week, just as we had when I was ill. I smiled back at her hopeful; maybe he would read me to sleep again.

I washed all the sheets and blankets we owned and had the guest rooms and Mormor's room ready upstairs. I took the wedding ring quilt out of my hope chest and laid it on the large bed in Mormor and Jorik's old room. I had not dared use it yet, but now it seemed appropriate for a master bedroom. Henry had moved to the cottage and the only thing left to work on was the baking for the company coming in two days. "Henry and I have been invited to the Crawley's for supper tonight so do not fix anything for us, my dear," Mormor said smiling. I nodded and sighed in fatigue without realizing it. "Your quilt looks beautiful in here," Mormor said approvingly.

"Thank you! It does fit the bed well," I said, appreciating the fresh look of the room.

"What is wrong, Georgie? Are you nervous for my family to come?" she asked.

I smiled weakly and nodded. "I hope Keane's family will approve of me. What if they are angry with him for not marrying Melody? But I suppose I am mostly worried about being under the same roof as Melody, knowing she and Keane were in love," I confessed.

Mormor hugged me to her side. "I can tell Keane has no feelings left for the girl after all she has done. He is in love with you," she said tenderly.

I shrugged. "He hasn't said those words yet, but I pray that he will someday," I confessed.

"He will, Georgie. Keane overthinks things; he always has. He is a serious young man at times, but he tries hard to make the right decisions and never takes them lightly. I honestly think he has been waiting to know for certain his heart is free before he gives it to you. That and perhaps a bit of stubbornness mixed in that I was right about you all along," Mormor said, trying to give me more insight on her grandson. "Well, Henry is waiting for me. You will be all alone for a few hours until Keane returns; you have been working too hard again. Why not take a hot bath and soak your sore muscles?" she suggested, smiling.

I smiled in return. "I do believe I will," I said, going to the kitchen to put water on to boil. The creek was too cold now as October was only a day away, but I missed those swimming days with Keane. I pulled the metal tub into the bedroom, and as the water boiled, I took my hair down and laid out my night clothes. It seemed so odd to have my things in drawers next to Keane's. After a few more kettles full of water, I climbed in and began to wash with the scented soaps my mother made. I soaked in the relaxing hot water, wondering what kinds of food Keane's family might enjoy. And, of course, we needed some kind of wedding cake. I could bake the cake but wasn't certain how good it would look. My baking was delectable but not fanciful in the least. Perhaps it wasn't too late to check with the bakery in one of the larger towns.

Suddenly, the back door swung open and the screen door slammed. I sat up alarmed, knowing I was home alone and had never thought to lock the doors. The bedroom door swung open, and I screamed as Keane blushed. "Georgiana, are you all right? Do you need a doctor?" he asked, panicked and walking toward me.

"I am fine. Why on earth would I need a doctor?" I asked, blushing and trying to sink lower it the bath suds.

"I met Mormor and Henry in town. She said you were not feeling well and that I needed to hurry home to check on you. I rode as fast as I could," he said breathlessly.

I gasped and blushed; *that ornery old woman.* Talk me into taking a bath and send Keane home running. I shook my head. "I feel fine."

He felt my forehead. "You are warm," he said, concerned.

I sighed. "I am in a hot bath; of course, my skin will be warm," I said, laughing. He looked embarrassed as he realized his precious Mormor was up to her old schemes again. "I left your supper on the back of the stove," I said, ready for him to leave. He nodded, thanked me, and then left the room.

I giggled as I stood to dry off, Mormor and her matchmaking. Wait until I figured out how to pay her back. She would be married in a few days' time; I wondered how she would like her grandchildren interfering?

Suddenly the door opened and shut. Keane stood leaning against it, looking in pain or perhaps frightened; I wasn't sure. "I can't think of eating just now, Georgiana," he said, swallowing hard. My heart raced as I realized Mormor might have known what she was doing after all.

CHAPTER NINE

The next day, I set out to do a few days' worth of baking. I sang hymns cheerfully as I worked. I had never been so happy in all my life. Mormor came into the kitchen and asked me how I had slept. I had to fight back a smile. "Perfectly! I had a nice long bath, read a book, and took a walk. I slept like a baby," I said, trying to throw her off with a little fib. She looked disappointed, and I smiled. *Serves the meddling old sweetheart right*, I thought silently. "What kind of wedding cake would you like?" I asked, punching down my bread dough.

"Oh, let's see. Just plain vanilla will do nicely, dear. It will just be immediate family, so no need to overdo it," she said, smiling. Keane and Henry were finishing the cottage, and tomorrow Keane's family would arrive. Friday afternoon Mormor and Henry would be wed, and Keane's family would leave on Saturday morning.

Dinner was ready, and I rang the bell to summon Henry and Keane from their work. "I can start moving some of your things over to the cottage, Ms. Addie, if you are ready," Henry said, smiling.

Mormor shook her head. "I told you, Henry, it's just Addie to you now."

Keane could not stop staring at me; I blushed and offered him more pie. He smiled and shook his head. "I will never refuse a second piece of your pie, my beautiful wife," he said with a mischievous grin.

Mormor glowed with happiness as she drank in her grandson's improved spirit. "I believe I *would* like to come and look at the progress on the cottage if you would walk me, Henry. Then I can tell you where I want the bigger items to go," she said, standing and taking her shawl off the coat rack hanging beside the door to the porch.

"Of course, my Addie," Henry said, offering his arm to his future bride.

"I will be there in a few minutes," Keane called after them.

Mormor waved him off. "Give us old lovebirds some time alone," she said, smiling.

Keane pulled me onto his lap and kissed me. "I love you, Georgiana, so much. I wish I had told you weeks ago, a month ago," he said sincerely.

"But you are telling me now, that is all that matters. I love you, Keane Kenrick, but I think you can call me Georgie now," I whispered in his ear.

He laughed. "No, I've changed my mind. You are too beautiful for Georgie, and everyone calls you Georgie. No, you will always be *my Georgiana*," he said, kissing me again. I smiled; I was so happy I felt my heart might burst at any moment.

"I have missed you all morning, *my wife*."

I smiled and laid my head on his chest. So this is what it felt like to be loved? Did I glow like Celia, Millie and Eleanor? "I had better finish this baking; I want to have enough to feed everyone."

"They will love you, do not worry," Keane said as if he could read my mind.

"I hope so." I wanted to please them for Keane's sake. I just prayed I was enough.

I looked out the window, fretting as the storm blew in. Keane and Mormor had driven the buggy into town to meet the train to pick up his family. Henry had driven the wagon to carry back their bags. I knew they would most likely stay in town and ride out the storm, but I hated being home alone with the fierce wind blowing in. It reminded me of the storm a month ago that had destroyed our crops and had taken our barn.

The house was clean and sparkling, the baking was done, and the wedding cake made and decorated to the best of my ability. I sat in the parlor at the piano, determined to calm my nerves. What would Melody look like? Would Keane take one look at her and wish he had married her instead even though she had betrayed him? I had given everything to him, and although I had never been happier, I felt a new sort of fragile vulnerability knowing my heart was no longer mine to control.

I held supper warming in the oven, checking it constantly so it didn't burn and dry out. I knew the cows would be restless needing to be milked, so I finally put on a long apron and work boots and held my skirts up as high as I could and tromped to the barn through the wind, rain and mud to tend to them.

I jumped at every noise in the barn as the wind roared outside and hurried through the milking as fast as I could. I had just come out of the barn when the carriage pulled up. Henry was in the wagon, old blankets covering the luggage. Keane was riding on the most beautiful black horse I had ever seen. I smiled brightly as my eyes met Keane's. Gaspard was home where he belonged, and the look on my husband's face caused my breath to catch in my chest. He was so handsome and happier than I had ever seen him before.

I was lugging the heavy pail of milk in one hand, my skirts dragging in the mud, my hair soaked. I looked dreadful I knew. Keane jumped down from Gaspard and rushed to me. "Oh,

Georgiana! I am so sorry. We had to wait at the diner because of the storm. Here, let me carry that for you. Come meet my family. This is Gaspard; he is finally home," he said, smiling.

"He is beautiful. Hello, Gaspard. Welcome to Kenrick Farms," I said, rubbing his nose gently.

I blushed as Keane helped me walk to where his family now waited. "Mother, Father, this is my wife, Georgiana. Georgiana, this is Jaffett and Leonora Kenrick, my parents," he said proudly.

Keane's father shook my hand and smiled, but his mother pulled me into a warm hug. "It is good to meet our new daughter," she said, smiling. Keane looked so much like his mother, their fair hair and dark blue eyes.

"Welcome to our home," I said nervously.

"And this is my younger brother Ian and his wife, Caterina, and this is Eitan and his new wife, Melody," Keane said, hugging me close. "Brothers, this is my beautiful wife, Georgiana." He sounded proud, and I felt my blush.

I greeted them as warmly as I could. Caterina seemed friendly though a little shy, but nothing prepared me for the lovely Melody. Her long coal black curls so perfectly framed a heart shaped face with large brown eyes and rosy cheeks. She looked like a porcelain doll, so dainty and feminine. I suddenly felt wretchedly ugly and plain as I welcomed them all.

Mormor took over and invited everyone inside. "Go on and clean up, Georgie; I will show everyone to their rooms," Mormor said, saving me. I thanked her and rushed inside to our room where I frowned at my appearance, and silently knew why it took Keane so long to get over Melody. She was perfectly beautiful.

I changed quickly into my silver-blue dress and tried to dry my hair the best I could. I finally gave up, brushed it, and tied it back with a white ribbon. "I am afraid if we do not eat soon, it will be ruined," I told Keane. He had just come in from settling Gaspard in the new stables and followed me into the kitchen. He smiled, kissed my cheek, and called his family into the formal dining room as Mormor and Leonora helped me carry the dishes of food in to serve.

As Keane led his family in a blessing, I silently prayed the roast beef wasn't overly done. I had expected to eat nearly two hours before. I listened as the family talked with Mormor and Keane, catching up on the latest happenings in Newbury where Keane had grown up. Keane told of our storm and losing our crops and barn and how he planned to expand into more acreage come spring. He told about the brood mare in Slatsville that he hoped to travel to see soon.

When I went into the kitchen to bring out the blackberry cobblers, Leonora came to help me. "I have never seen Keane look so happy before. Thank you, Georgiana. You are good for him and it shows."

I blushed. "I love him, very much," I assured her. I quickly said no more as Caterina and Melody came in to help bring coffee cups. Both women were expecting, although it was common knowledge now that Melody's child was by another man. She had intended to trick Keane into a quick marriage to cover her sins, and when he came to Crawford and married me, she knew she had to do something quickly. She betrayed Eitan into thinking the child was Keane's, and he married her to protect their family name. Once the doctor confirmed her pregnancy, Eitan and his family knew she had betrayed them. Keane had been terribly hurt that Eitan would think him capable of doing such a terrible thing. Melody's father was a wealthy banker and had offered Eitan a high position at his bank if he would agree to remain married to his daughter and raise her child. I wondered if the job was worth it, for neither Melody nor Eitan looked happy.

"I do not know how you can stand living out here. It is so far from town, and look at you, you have to work so hard," Melody said, turning her nose up at me. Caterina looked shocked.

I felt my face warming. "I love farm life. I am blessed to live on Kenrick Farms. I adore it," I said softly.

Melody shook her head of ebony curls and sighed. "I suppose God makes all kinds of women. The soft and elegant kind and the women built for hard labor," she said spitefully.

Caterina shook her head at Melody, warning her. "Serve the coffee now, Melody," she said firmly. Melody sashayed out of the room, and I sighed in relief.

"Ignore her; we all do," Caterina said, smiling weakly. I nodded and followed her into the dining room with a tray of coffee cups.

"This cobbler is wonderful, Georgiana," Ian and Jaffett both complimented. I blushed and thanked them.

Keane smiled proudly. "Georgiana is a wonderful cook. Her baking is famous in Crawford," he bragged. I couldn't help but notice the scowl on Melody's face; neither could Mormor as she gave me a wink.

After dinner, the women helped clean up. We retired to the parlor where Mormor asked me to play for them. Henry took out his harmonica, and to our surprise, Eitan rushed and brought back his violin. He played beautifully, and before long, I begged to just sit and listen, in awe of his talent. But Melody did not look impressed by her husband's abilities, but merely bored. Caterina stood and made her excuses to retire for the night; she was expecting in four months and was fatigued from their journey. I asked her if she would like a bath, but she said perhaps tomorrow morning.

"Well, I would like my bath tonight," Melody said, standing. As I rushed to heat water on the stove, she crossed her arms impatiently. "I cannot believe you have to do all of this just to bathe! Why do you not have running water?" she demanded.

"We have an indoor pump," I offered, thinking she needed a cold bath to cool her demeanor.

"Humph! I will wait for the hot water, thank you. Just bring it up to my room when it is ready," she insisted.

"We do not have a tub upstairs, but you can use our room for privacy," I offered. Mormor found us and smiled warmly. I tried my best to smile back.

"Can you not hurry that water up?" Melody asked, pouting.

Mormor smiled. "I can take you down to the creek; it is much faster to bathe there," she offered. I turned to hide my smile.

"I would rather die than bathe in filthy creek water," Melody said sourly.

"It is good you did not marry Ian or Keane then, for this is the life of farmers," Mormor said firmly. If looks could kill, Mormor and I both would be six feet under with the scowls Melody was giving us.

I got her settled into her bath and whispered to Keane not to go anywhere near the kitchen or our room. I watched the clock for what seemed like an hour and wondered how long one could possibly stay in the bath? I was tired and ready for everyone to retire. Mormor and Leonora once again saved me by checking on Melody and helping her; she had been waiting for someone to dress her as if we were her maids.

Leonora bid us all a good night, taking Melody upstairs with her. I took Keane's hand in mine and squeezed it tenderly. "I will leave you men to catch up; I am tired as well," I whispered and then said my goodnights. I quickly washed up and dressed for bed. I lay awake listening as the men's voices echoed from the parlor. I liked Keane's family, all except Melody, but I would do my best to be civil and gracious, making her stay a pleasant one. I had to, at least for two more days.

I rose extra early the next morning to fry potatoes, onions, and bacon. I hurried to make biscuits and milk gravy from the bacon drippings. I had made up several dozen cinnamon rolls, and I hoped between the varieties of foods there would be something each one would enjoy. Keane kissed me as he came in from the barn. "Keane! Someone will walk in and see us," I giggled.

"You were asleep by the time I came to bed last night. I miss being able to talk to you before I fall asleep," he whispered.

I looked him in the eyes and found myself blushing. "I miss that, too," I whispered.

"I love you so much, Georgiana. I am glad to see my family, but I am ready to have you all to myself," he said, smiling.

I hugged him tightly. "Go away and let me do my chores, Husband," I scolded, and he laughed warmly. "How was Gaspard this morning?" I asked, knowing how proud he was to have him home in our new stable.

Keane flashed that breathtaking smile of his and nodded. "He looked like he adjusted well. I cannot wait until we can travel to

Slatsville to see the brood mare. We will make a trip of it," he said with a wink.

I smiled in surprise. "You are going to take me along?" I asked.

He pulled me into his arms tenderly. "I cannot be away from you, not for a day, not for an hour. I want you to come with me," he said, kissing me just as his parents cleared their throats. I blushed and rushed to get their plates of breakfast.

They both complimented me on breakfast. Ian and Eitan came in, and Keane joined them in the dining room. Henry was next and then Mormor. "After breakfast I will show you the new barn and stables," Keane said to his brothers as I brought in more coffee. "Georgiana, sit with me and eat," he said, taking my free hand. Looking around to make certain everyone was served, I nodded and left to get my own plate.

"Georgiana tends to work too hard," I could hear Mormor complain.

I smiled to myself and was startled as Caterina came in. "Oh, good morning, Caterina. What would you like to eat this morning?" I asked, showing her the variety of foods.

"A little of everything please; it all looks so delicious," she said, giggling. I helped her to the dining room and served her tea and returned for my own things.

"This is wonderful, Georgiana," Eitan complimented, and everyone quickly agreed.

"Yes Son, you have found the perfect farm wife," Jaffett said, smiling. It was meant to be a compliment, but I remembered what Melody had said the day before, that God made some women for hard work. Did that mean I wasn't pretty and that I was manly in some way? I looked at Caterina, and though she showed with child, she was lovely with her dark brown hair and green eyes. Caterina had married Ian, and they ran her family farm. If Caterina was so lovely and yet a farm wife, then perhaps I shouldn't worry and just be proud to be Keane's farm wife.

Hearing a crash in the kitchen, I jumped up to see what it was. Keane followed me. Melody was standing in the middle of a broken jar of apple butter. My first instinct was to laugh, but I quickly began to wipe her off as Keane picked up shards of glass.

"What happened?" Keane asked her.

"I cannot eat any of this.….I was going to make myself some toast but with one taste of this apple butter, I was so shocked at how sour it was, I dropped the entire jar to the floor. It is inedible," she insisted. I gasped. Had my apple butter gone bad in the cellar somehow?

"No one has ever said a bad word against Georgiana's apple butter or her cooking for that matter. It was not sour when I ate it just minutes ago," Keane said in my defense.

"It is terrible; I shall starve to death at this rate," she complained.

"I will make your toast. Go on and join Eitan in the dining room," I said, sighing and cleaning up the rest of the mess.

"Do not listen to her, Georgiana. I love your apple butter; so does Henry and Mormor. You do not have to cater to her," Keane said tenderly. I thanked him and went to slice a loaf of bread. Out of all my cooking that morning and the days before, the spoiled little brat wanted toast. I had to quote the Beatitudes from the Bible to calm myself down and quickly repented.

I boiled water all morning for baths. If we did well on crops next year, perhaps I could talk Keane into indoor tubs with running water. I was so busy working, helping, and directing, and then starting the large amount of food for dinner, that I had no time to work on my own appearance. Apparently the smell of my cooking made Melody sick, and I again had to quote scripture to calm myself as I made her a simple bowl of oatmeal. Caterina helped me do the dishes, and soon it was time to dress for the wedding. I quickly dressed in my wedding dress and boots. Not having time to curl my hair, I braided both sides and twisted both braids around my head forming a halo and leaving the rest of my long hair hanging down my back. It was the best I could do in such a short time.

Keane came in and dressed in his wedding attire and pulled me close. "You are holding up wonderfully. Mother and Father adore you already. I am so proud you are my wife," he said, kissing me. I smiled and was thankful they accepted me. I enjoyed spending time with them and thought I could even get close to Caterina but found myself still trying to pacify Melody, and not liking her one bit. Perhaps I was jealous and holding a grudge. I needed to pray through on that. I asked God to help me as Melody called for someone to iron her dress for her.

Pastor Crawley and his wife arrived and joined us in the parlor where the marriage ceremony would take place. Eitan played his violin softly, and a new happiness glowed on Mormor's face as Jaffett gave her away to Henry. I could not help my tears of joy, and they only intensified when Keane held me to his side tenderly. Three months ago I would never have imagined being so in love and happy with Keane. Henry kissed Mormor while everyone clapped and cheered. We went into the dining room for wedding cake and coffee with Pastor Crawley and his wife.

Later, we began setting tables up outside for the reception we were hosting that evening for Mormor and Henry. Nearly half the town of Crawford was invited. When my family arrived, I hugged them excitedly. My mother stepped back and looked at me, sensing a change in her oldest daughter. "Everything looks to be going wonderful for you, Georgiana. You are glowing!" she said, smiling.

I nodded and hugged her tight. "I am very happy," I said, blushing. My sisters all hugged me and began to help carry out plates of food and bouquets of wildflowers, the last of the season, to decorate the tables. One by one, the wagons and buggies arrived; our small community was here to help us celebrate Henry and Mormor's marriage.

The music began, and I squealed as Keane twirled me onto our new wooden barn floor. Keane was so happy; I was proud to call him my husband. I saw Eleanor and Millie smiling at me from a distance. They winked; apparently my happiness was noticeable to more than just my mother. Eitan insisted on the next dance with me; Ian the next, and Jaffett, my father-in-law soon after. It was a wonderful evening of celebration; God had richly blessed so many of us.

Robert had come with Dr. Childers, and Keane held his temper remarkably. Although as I danced by with Robert, I could see he wasn't happy, but he was trying to overcome his jealousy. My sister Valynn handed me a cup of lemonade as Robert took a turn on the dance floor with Celia.

I thanked her but looked around for Keane. I hoped he wasn't upset with me for dancing with Robert or sulking somewhere still jealous. "I wonder where Keane went?" I asked Valynn as my eyes searched the entire barn.

Her cheeks turned red. "He followed Melody out of the barn while you danced with Robert," she whispered as if she shouldn't be telling me anything at all.

"Oh!" I said, fighting my own jealously just a bit. "He must be helping her find something," I said softly.

"He doesn't like it when you dance with Robert," she whispered again.

I nodded. "Perhaps I will help him and Melody," I said, handing her my cup and forcing a smile as I left the barn. I looked around the dimly lit yard trying to see them. Having no luck, I went into the house, quietly listening for voices and wondering if perhaps I had missed them outside. I had just turned to leave when I saw them, together, in our room, kissing. I gasped out loud, and Keane looked up angrily and shoved Melody back. My mind was whirling, the room was now spinning, and my heart was completely broken.

"Georgiana, it is not what you think!" Keane yelled and pushed by Melody who was grabbing at his shirt.

I had nowhere to go; people were everywhere outside and Keane and Melody in my room. I ran into the old guest room that was now Keane's study and locked the door. Burying my face in my hands, I sobbed as Keane banged on the door for me to let him in. "Go away!" I screamed at him.

"Georgiana, you know me! I would never do this to you. She tricked me; I swear it!" Keane yelled angrily.

"Do not lie to her, Keane; you have never been able to keep your hands off me," I heard Melody say seductively behind him.

"Get off me, you tramp! Get back out to that barn and tell your husband you are leaving, tonight. Now!" he screamed. I shook. I had never heard him so angry before. My mind struggled with sorting the truth of what I saw, with what I knew of Keane, but I couldn't think. I couldn't breathe. "Georgiana, I must speak with you. I have to see you. Please open the door!" Keane begged me. I sat in the corner of the room and lay my head against the wall; my entire world had just caved in on me.

"What is going on in here?" I heard Jaffett demand on the other side of the door.

"Melody came to me in the barn, said she needed help reaching something in the kitchen for Mormor. I followed her in, not suspecting anything, and she shoved me into my bedroom and threw herself on me, kissing me. Georgiana walked in just as I was shoving her away. But Georgiana will not let me explain; she will not let me in," Keane said, sounding frantic.

"Melody, explain yourself," Leonora said firmly. I could hear Melody's dramatics as she gave the opposite of Keane's encounter, saying he enticed her to follow him into our room. I held my hands over my ears not able to listen anymore.

"Melody, you promised when we agreed to bring you that you would do nothing to destroy Keane's marriage." This was surprisingly from the quiet Caterina.

"How do you know she isn't telling the truth this time? We all know how Keane feels about her?" Eitan said, and I could tell this was hurting him as well.

"She never tells the truth, Eitan. How many times has she lied to us? And you can see how happy Keane is now; he never looked that way with Melody," Ian insisted.

"Where is my daughter? Where is Georgiana?" I heard my mother ask, concerned. I rushed to the door.

"Please, Mrs. Andley, please talk her into letting me in. I have to see her! I have to explain. She must believe me!" Keane pleaded, the emotion in his voice breaking my heart.

"I will try my best, Keane," Mother said tenderly. She knocked; I let her in and quickly locked the door back. Crying, I threw myself into her arms. Mother held me and let me cry and then whispered, "You need to speak with your husband. You cannot lock yourself away every time a trial comes."

I shook my head. "I cannot look at him, not after seeing them together, in our room, kissing. I gave him everything, Mother; I should have known he still loves her," I said, sobbing.

"I think you owe it to him to listen. He is desperate to see you; I do not think he would be if he were guilty," she whispered. I could still hear his family squabbling outside the door. "From what you have told me of this girl, she doesn't seem trustworthy. But so far, Keane has proven he is honest. Hasn't he?" Mother asked me.

I closed my eyes. He had kept himself from me for over three months, told me he loved another from the beginning, and did not fully seek me until he knew he was over her. He had made certain his heart was free before claiming mine. "Yes, Keane is honest," I nodded, realizing the truth so strongly now. "I just need some time alone to sort this out. I am so embarrassed. I cannot get the image of them together out of my head. May I go home with you? Just for tonight? I can't be here with him, with her. Just one night, Mother?" I pleaded.

"Oh, Georgie, sweetheart! I cannot watch you hurt so. You may come home, but one night only. You must speak with

Keane alone before we leave; you must hear him out. I will tell your father to ready the carriage," Mother said, wavering in her willingness to let me leave my problems behind.

"I will speak with Keane in here; I do not want to face everyone out there," I said. I was now ashamed I had locked myself in a room like a child, a heartbroken child.

Mother kissed my forehead and stepped out of the room. "Please send your family back to the barn. Georgiana will speak with you in the study," I heard Mother say to Keane softly.

"You heard her, everyone to the barn. Eitan, I want your wife to stay away from my wife. There is a hotel in town; I will pay for your room if you will consent to go tonight," I heard Keane say bitterly. I knew I had handled this terribly. Now his family would resent me; they would feel obligated to leave and miss spending the remainder of their time with Mormor and their son.

The door opened and Keane rushed toward me. I had never seen that look in his eyes, *the look of a lost little boy.* "Georgiana," he said, trying to hold me, but I stepped away from him.

"I am trying to sort this all out, Keane. I do believe Melody tricked you, but I am so hurt seeing you kissing her," I said, trembling.

His eyes filled with tears. "I did not kiss her back. There is a difference. You know me, Georgiana; surely you know I would never do this to you. Never, especially now that we have shared....*I love you desperately!*" he said, so full of intense emotion.

"I am going home with my parents, Keane, just for tonight. I need time to think, to work..."

He cut me off falling to his knees before me. "Do not leave me, Georgiana, I beg you. Search your heart. You know I couldn't do this to you. I have waited all this time for you. I love you. You are my everything. I need you; please do not leave!" he pleaded so desperately it almost frightened me. "I only want *you*, please, believe me." I turned my back. I couldn't watch his agony, for now it seemed to overpower my own pain; and then he was behind me, holding me. "I cannot live without you; I cannot lose you after I just found you," he said, kissing my head, my cheek, and my neck. I turned and held him closely, tears streaming down my cheeks as he kissed me, whispering he loved me desperately. It was in that moment I knew I could not leave my husband, not even for one night. I had waited all these months, and I was finally loved, and I loved him deeply in return.

"I will not leave you," I whispered through my tears.

I walked out of the room holding onto Keane's arm and was relieved that only our parents remained in the house. "I want to stay here, at home," I said, hugging my mother and smiling though my eyes were still red and swollen. She smiled and nodded that I had made the right choice.

My father hugged me tightly. "I love you, Daughter," he whispered emotionally. I knew he ached to comfort me, to take my pain as his own.

"I love you, Father," I said, kissing his cheek. I looked to Keane's father and mother. "I am sorry I handled this so poorly. I do wish for all of you to stay, just as planned until your train departs tomorrow. I would love more time to visit with you, and I know Keane does as well. And please tell Eitan and Melody they are also welcome to stay," I said, burying the pain her name still brought to me.

Leonora hugged me closely. "You are such a strong and good woman, the best choice as a wife for our Keane. We are thankful he has you. We would love to stay and spend more time with you both," she said, pulling Keane into our embrace. Keane held me closely; he wasn't going to let me go for a second. I suppose he was afraid I would change my mind and leave with my parents.

"Does everyone in the barn know then?" I asked, trying to decide what to do with our guests.

My mother shook her head no. "Only the family knows; everyone else is dancing with Adeline and Henry and having a wonderful time," she assured me.

I nodded and drew in a deep breath. "I do not feel like facing a crowd...," I started, knowing my face was terribly splotchy and swollen.

"I will announce you have a headache, and we will stay and help clean up. You go on and lie down. Keane, help her get settled and then come on out with us," my mother said, taking charge.

I was thankful when everyone left us. I went into our room and Keane helped me change into my nightgown and tucked me into our bed. "I will hurry back," he whispered. "Please, Georgiana, do not leave me, never leave me," he pleaded into my neck as he held me.

I sighed and smiled weakly. "I will not leave, Keane, I cannot; I love you too much," I whispered. He kissed me passionately. I felt his love so deeply it hurt.

"I will hurry back," he promised. I nodded, but soon after he left me, I fell fast asleep, secure in his love for me.

The next morning I rose early to make breakfast. Keane's family would be leaving in just a few hours, and I could not help but feel a little relieved. Leonora and Caterina soon joined me, helping to serve the men as they came in from checking on Gaspard. "Son, I am proud of the life you are building here. Father Jorik is smiling down from heaven, I am certain of it," Jaffett said with emotion in his eyes as he thought of his father.

"Thank you, Father," Keane said, touched.

"We will miss you, of course, but you must promise to visit as often as you can, especially once our grandchildren start arriving," Jaffett said, causing Keane and me both to blush. Keane assured him we would try to visit soon after the first of the year.

When Henry and Mormor joined us, I could see the pride in Mormor's eyes as she kissed each of her family members goodbye. "Henry and I want to be there for the birth of our first great-grandchild," Mormor assured Ian and Caterina. Ian hugged his grandmother warmly and wished her and Henry happiness.

"I want to tell you how brave you are, and I am so glad we are sisters now. I wish it were you in Newbury instead of Melody. But please come as soon as you can to visit," Caterina said, hugging me in the kitchen.

I blushed, still embarrassed by the way I handled the night before. "We will; I promise. Perhaps after your baby comes we can visit," I said, thanking her.

"And perhaps your own little one will be on the way by then as well," she said, smiling warmly. I hugged her close.

"I hope so," I whispered. I smiled, and for the first time realized she might be right. A new joy filled my heart at the prospect of having my own baby by this time next year.

Keane put his arm around me as we stood on the front porch and waved goodbye to his family. "Did you and Eitan make up?" I asked softly, knowing he had been troubled all morning by his brother's comments the night before.

Keane nodded. "He apologized, and I forgave him. But he has to live with her now which will be the hard part. He told me in the barn this morning that he had always been rather jealous of me, and when Melody approached him seductively and fed him the lies that she carried my child, he had wanted to show me he could have something of mine," Keane said, sighing and pulling me closer.

"Poor Eitan!" I said, laying my head against Keane's chest and hugging him close.

"Yes, poor Eitan. Only God can help them now," Keane said wisely.

"We will pray for them," I whispered. He kissed my forehead and lifted my chin so that my eyes met his.

"I do not deserve you, Georgiana. I have fought this love for you so hard. Do not ask me why, for I do not know. I look at you and think, what a fool I have been, but I had to be certain my heart was yours completely. I made a promise to you. I would never break your heart on purpose, so I had to be sure. Every day you have won my heart with your smile, your beauty, your adorable personality but mostly your beautiful heart. I cannot tell you how frightened I was last night that you were leaving me, that you didn't believe me. I didn't want to live without you. I realized just how much you have come to mean to me. I can never withhold my love from you, and I can never be away from you. *You* are my future, Georgiana, my dream, not the farm, not the horses. *You*, my beautiful wife; *I must have you, always*," he whispered.

"Keane, I love you so very much," I whispered, kissing him with a love that overwhelmed me, a love I never dreamt I would have. And for the first time, I felt I was enough.

EPILOGUE

October 29ᵗʰ, the following year....

"It is time! The baby will be here by the morning!" Keane called into the kitchen excitedly.

I gasped in surprise and wiped my hands on my apron as I lay aside my baking. "Is she doing well?" I asked, slipping my shawl around my shoulders and smiling at the excitement on my husband's face. We had long awaited this day; it had finally arrived, the beginning of Keane's dream.

He hugged me closely and then laughed as my oversized stomach got in the way. He placed his hands on either side and smiled. "Do you hear that, little one? Armenta is going to foal!" he said, making me laugh. My heart swelled with love as he talked to our soon-coming child.

Hand and hand we walked excitedly to the stables. Henry and the new veterinarian from town were with Armenta, our beautiful grey Percheron mare. Mormor hugged me closely and kissed my cheek. "Should you be out in this chilly air so close to your time?" she asked, concerned.

I smiled. "I cannot miss this!" I insisted nervously. Minutes turned into hours as we eagerly awaited our first foal at Kenrick Farms Stables.

"Hey, I wondered where everyone had run off to; thought I missed the rapture or something." I heard and turned to hug my younger sister Valynn.

"Armenta is foaling," I whispered.

Her beautiful blue eyes lit up excitedly. "I am here in time then," she said, pleased. Valynn was coming to stay with me for the next few weeks as my first child was due. I sat down on a milking stool, no longer able to bear the weight on my back.

"Who is that man with Henry?" Valynn whispered with a wistful look on her face.

I looked surprised; Valynn had been courting Isaac Stein for nearly a year. "That is Dr. McCray, the town's first veterinarian," I whispered in return but watched my sister closely. Soon I had to stand, my back hurting terribly. Keane pulled me closely and leaned me back against him. Valynn brought out mugs of hot coffee and the cinnamon rolls I had baked earlier in the day.

"Poor Armenta!" I said, hating to watch the mare suffer so.

"Georgiana, it is getting late. This could take hours still. Go on to bed, and I will wake you when the foal is here," Keane whispered tenderly.

"Just a little while longer, then I will retire," I promised with a smile. I didn't have to wait much longer.

"Here it comes!" Dr. McCray said excitedly. Keane rushed to help while I anxiously hugged Valynn and Mormor to my side. We all three cried tears of joy as Armenta delivered her first foal, a filly, a beautiful black filly, strong and healthy. Keane and Henry looked like proud papas about to burst with joy, patting each other on the back, hugging Dr. McCray.

Keane rushed to me and hugged me closely. "A filly, Georgiana! We have a filly! The first foal of Kenrick Farms Stables, and she is a beauty!" he gushed overjoyed. We watched quietly as Armenta got her baby up on wobbly legs, and the foal began to nurse.

"What will we call her?" Henry asked, hugging Mormor and smiling like he had just been made a grandpa.

Keane looked to me. "Ophelia of Gaspard!" I said proudly. Keane rushed to get his farm log book where he kept track of the horse's information. I watched as he proudly logged in our first foal: her name, sire, dame, and her birth date. Suddenly a pain struck through my aching back and into my stomach. I gasped and held onto Valynn for support.

"Georgie!" Mormor and Valynn both called out in fear. Keane stood up from the table and looked concerned. Suddenly a whoosh sounded as my water broke and covered the barn floor beneath my skirts. I nearly collapsed.

"Georgie!" Valynn called out, frightened.

"Well, Mr. Kenrick, it looks as if you will need Dr. Childers' services now, two births in one day. How did you get so lucky?" Dr. McCray asked smiling brightly.

Keane looked pale as he walked toward me, but I could not read his face. Suddenly all six foot two inches of my husband sank to the barn floor in a dead faint. "Keane!" I screamed.

Henry and Mormor rushed to him as Dr. McCray knelt beside my husband trying to bring him to.

"Come on, Georgie, let's get you into the house and cleaned up. You do not want to wait as long as Celia did," Valynn said with a chuckle. My sister had waited nearly too long to send for Dr. Childers, and my poor bother-in-law and we four sisters nearly delivered baby Johnny ourselves. "You will ride for the doctor, Henry," I heard Valynn say in her best commanding voice.

"I will be happy to go for him, Miss Andley," Dr. McCray said cheerfully.

Valynn flashed him her prettiest smile and thanked him. "Come along, Georgie. We have a baby to deliver," she said sweetly.

Two Hours Later....

"What are you doing here? Where is Dr. Childers?" I heard my husband ask, and I groaned.

"He is attending to Mary Beth Winter's pneumonia. He will be over as soon as he is done," I heard Robert Anderson assure Keane.

"You will wait for him if you can," Keane instructed.

Robert came in smiling and sighed. "I hope you do not send me away, Georgie. I might be your last resort unless you want me to bring Dr. McCray back. I am sure a veterinarian could assist," Robert teased lightly. I groaned in pain, and at that point I did not care who helped me.

My mother came in shortly after and Mormor on her heels with towels and fresh linens. "Can you believe two births in one day, first the foal and now my grandchild?" my mother said, smiling proudly.

"It is a day to mark down in the history of Kenrick Farms," Mormor said even prouder.

Another contraction came and Robert looked alarmed. "I do not think you will make it until Dr. Childers arrives, Georgie. That contraction was exactly two minutes from the last," he said and began to set up the room and give orders. Valynn and Mother carried in hot water. Mormor wiped my face with a cool cloth.

Robert quickly left the room. "Mr. Kenrick, it will not be much longer; I cannot wait for Dr. Childers," I heard Robert say softly outside the door.

I heard Keane sigh in defeat. "Please let me go to her," Keane pleaded.

"It is best if you wait here. They say you fainted in the barn earlier; I dare say you would again," I heard Robert chuckle.

"Just help her, Dr. Anderson; help Georgiana," Keane pleaded softly. Robert seemed relieved when he came back in and quickly examined me.

"Georgiana, can you hear me?" I heard my husband call through the bedroom door.

I smiled through my pain. "Yes Keane, I can hear you," I said, not as loudly as I had hoped to.

"I love you, Georgiana. I love you."

Tears filled my eyes. "Keane, I love you, too. Now go away so I can concentrate," I said as another contraction came. I could not hold back my scream on this one.

"All right, Georgie, we must do this together, just two old friends," Robert said, trying to take the awkwardness out of the situation. I nodded; I no longer cared. "When I tell you to push, I need you to push with all you have," he said rather nervously. I nodded. Mother kissed my cheek, and Mormor prayed softly. Just minutes later I lay exhausted as Robert held up my baby and smiled brightly. "It is a girl, Georgie! She is perfect in every way!"

Mormor praised God, and Mother wept as she helped Robert clean the baby and wrap her quickly in the soft yellow blanket I had made for this day. As they laid my daughter in my arms, I could not stop my tears. I had never seen anything so beautiful. "Hello there, little one," I whispered emotionally. Valynn stood next to me and cried her own tears of joy.

"She is beautiful, Georgie," Mother said tenderly.

I nodded. "She is perfect. And she is mine. *I love her so*," I whispered through my tears.

"If you ladies will help me clean this lovely woman up, I think her husband will be most anxious to join her," Robert said tenderly.

My eyes met his, and I smiled. "Thank you," I said softly. He nodded and smiled.

Just a few minutes later Robert left the room, and through the door I could hear him announce to Keane, Henry, Genevieve, Augusta, and my father that we had a perfect baby girl.

"Is Georgiana all right?" Keane asked softly.

"Yes, she did excellent. Fastest birth I have attended. You may go and see them now," Robert said.

My heart ached as Keane walked in, tears in his eyes. He rushed to me and held me to his chest. "Thank you, God!" he whispered emotionally. He kissed me tenderly and looked down into the face of our baby girl. "She is beautiful, and she has your nose," he chuckled softly.

I smiled. It was too early to tell these things, but he was so sweet. "Do you want to hold her?" I asked. He nodded, and I gently placed her in his strong arms.

"What will you call her?" my mother asked.

I smiled at Keane. "Jori Adeline Kenrick," I said proudly.

Mormor burst into tears, and Keane wept as well. "Jorik is watching from heaven, and he is proud," Mormor said through her tears. I smiled through tears of my own and nodded; I could feel Jorik Kenrick's presence so strongly.

As Keane handed our precious bundle back to me, I couldn't help but smile. A year ago I could never have imagined my life turning out so beautifully. But it had. All of my dreams had come true, and they were right within my arms reach, both of them.

The End

TO MY READERS

I hope you have enjoyed reading *Georgiana*, Book One of The Andley Sisters Series. Be looking for the other three books in this series coming soon! Also being released in the fall of 2016 is *Estelle*, Book One of The Royals of Gliston Series. Your feedback is very important to me. Please find me on Goodreads, Amazon, or from one of the social media links below, and leave me a comment.

Be blessed,

Sherri Beth Johnson

Website: www.sherribethjohnson.wordpress.com

Email: sherribethjohnson@gmail.com

Facebook: www.facebook.com/sherribethjohnson

Instagram: sbethjohnson41

Twitter: @sbethjohnson

Pinterest: sbjAuthor

54055960R00108

Made in the USA
Lexington, KY
31 July 2016